SPECIAL MESSAGE TO READERS

THE ULVERSCROFT FOUNDATION
(registered UK charity number 264873)

was established in 1972 to provide funds for research, diagnosis and treatment of eye diseases. Examples of major projects funded by the Ulverscroft Foundation are:-

- The Children's Eye Unit at Moorfields Eye Hospital, London
- The Ulverscroft Children's Eye Unit at Great Ormond Street Hospital for Sick Children
- Funding research into eye diseases and treatment at the Department of Ophthalmology, University of Leicester
- The Ulverscroft Vision Research Group, Institute of Child Health
- Twin operating theatres at the Western Ophthalmic Hospital, London
- The Chair of Ophthalmology at the Royal Australian College of Ophthalmologists

You can help further the work of the Foundation by making a donation or leaving a legacy. Every contribution is gratefully received. If you would like to help support the Foundation or require further information, please contact:

THE ULVERSCROFT FOUNDATION
The Green, Bradgate Road, Anstey
Leicester LE7 7FU, England
Tel: (0116) 236 4325

website: www.foundation.ulverscroft.com

DISTRICT NURSE

Desperate for a change to her humdrum routine, Helen Barclay accepts the post of district nurse and moves to the Norfolk countryside with her mother to take care of patients in several villages. They both soon settle in, and are happy with their new circumstances. Then two men enter Helen's life. One brings a host of dark emotions that threaten to confuse her, and the other seems to be just what she needs . . . but is he?

Books by Phyllis Mallett
in the Linford Romance Library:

LOVE IN PERIL
THE TURNING POINT
LOVE'S MASQUERADE
POOR LITTLE RICH GIRL
ISLE OF INTRIGUE
HOUSE OF FEAR
DEADLY INHERITANCE
THE HEART IS TORN
SINISTER ISLE OF LOVE
MISTRESS OF SEABROOK
HER SEARCHING HEART
TIDES OF LOVE
INTRIGUE IN ROME
DANGEROUS LOVE
IMPETUOUS NURSE
NURSE ON SKIS
PATIENT NURSE
MARRIED TO MEDICINE
DOCTOR'S DESTINY
EMERGENCY NURSE

PHYLLIS MALLETT

DISTRICT NURSE

Complete and Unabridged

LINFORD
Leicester

First published in Great Britain in 1969

First Linford Edition
published 2018

A catalogue record for this book is available from the British Library.

ISBN 978–1–4448–3906–7

Published by
F. A. Thorpe (Publishing)
Anstey, Leicestershire

Set by Words & Graphics Ltd.
Anstey, Leicestershire
Printed and bound in Great Britain by
T. J. International Ltd., Padstow, Cornwall

This book is printed on acid-free paper

1

Helen Barclay paused at the garden gate and glanced back at the new bungalow, with its neat little patch of lawn in front and flourishing flower beds. But her eyes were attracted to the bold sign on the post beside the hedge. DISTRICT NURSE. She breathed deeply as she waved to her mother peering from the window. They had finished moving in, and in the morning she would be assuming her duties as nurse for the district. But first there were several calls to make, and until they were safely behind her she could not relax enough to enjoy the pleasant Norfolk countryside in general or the little village of Bullingham in particular.

Ever since she had begun training as a very raw student nurse years before she had wanted to be a district nurse, living in the country in the freshness of nature, but until now she had been unable to fulfil her ambition. She didn't doubt that her widowed mother would find it difficult settling down in the country after so many years of living in London. But they were both adaptable, and Helen's heart seemed to swell with pleasure as she walked along the lane in beautiful May sunshine. There were birds singing in the thick hedges and the air was pure and healthy. This was the place to live! It was much simpler than the bustle of a general hospital in London. Life would be quieter and slower, and here she could forget about Harold and his influence of several years. He was going to marry an heiress, and if he didn't settle down to a life of squandering money then he would set himself up as a consultant in some fashionable practice. She was pleased that she had seen the light before it had been too late!

Bullingham was a widely scattered village, the centre of which were two shops and a public house on the main road, with no more than seven houses around them; and a larger area of a house or bungalow here and there encompassing something like three square miles. The nearest doctor was in the neighbouring market town of Truston, seven miles away, and Helen came under his jurisdiction. Norwich lay fifteen miles away, and Helen had already fallen in love with that fine old city.

She gazed around with eyes seeing simple pleasures for the first time. There were cows grazing in a meadow in front of a picturesque old farmhouse, a tractor busy spraying something on a field of fresh green sproutings, and the wide vista of fields added to the pleasure of solitude that came to her. Helen felt really at peace within for the first time in months. At last she had arrived, and now she was here she would enjoy life to the full. She didn't believe the words of most of the friends and acquaintances she'd left behind in the big city. Perhaps most of them would get bored and lost in a place like

Bullingham, but none of them was Helen Barclay, and she loved this rustic life.

Voices came to her ears and she paused and peered through a leafy hedge. She caught a glimpse of blue and red, and frowned when she heard splashing sounds. A little farther on was a gateway, and she walked to it and peered into the field, seeing immediately three very small children playing by a pond. The children seemed very young to be trusted near water unsupervized, and Helen lifted her gaze and searched for a sign of an adult. When she failed to see anyone who might be in charge of the children she opened the gate and went into the field. The joyous shouting of the children, two little girls and a boy, faded when they became aware of her presence, and they stood staring at her with wide, distrustful eyes as she approached.

'Hello,' Helen said, smiling gently. 'Do your mothers know you're here by the pond?'

'We mustn't come here,' came the hesitant reply from the little boy. He was thin and muddy, and his pale blue eyes stared at Helen from a small, freckled face. He had a shock of the reddest hair Helen had ever seen.

'What's your name?' Helen demanded.

'Tommy Brace,' came the defiant reply. 'Who are you? You don't live here.'

'I do now,' Helen told him, smiling. 'I'm the new District Nurse. I live in the bungalow called *Wistaria* in Thompson's Lane.'

'That's where Nurse Griffin lives,' said one of the little girls.

'Not any more.' Helen dropped to one knee in the tall grass and took the girl's hand. What's your name?'

'Mary James.' Brown eyes stared boldly into Helen's blue ones.

'And what's your name?' Helen looked at the other little girl.

'Shan't tell,' came the stiff reply. 'Mum told me not to speak to strangers.'

'And quite right, too!' Helen laughed as she got to her feet. 'But won't you show me where you live and I'll walk you home. It's dangerous to play so near to water. That pond looks rather deep, and I'm sure you're not old enough to know how to swim.'

'Don't tell my mother I've been here,' young Tommy said. 'I'll get the belt if you do.'

'Perhaps I won't if you promise me you won't come here again,' Helen retorted. 'Come along, and show me where you live.' She had already seen the red roofs of a group of council houses along the road, and she guessed that was where the children had come from.

The two girls obediently took Helen's hands and walked at her side, but the boy hung back, and when Helen turned to call to him she saw a man appearing from around a large bush beyond the pond. He called loudly to them, and at once the boy started running towards the gate. Helen caught him as he tried to pass her, and she held his hand until the newcomer arrived.

'What's going on here?' The man was in his early thirties, tall and broad shouldered, with brown eyes and a mass of unruly black hair hanging over his broad forehead. Didn't you see that notice about trespassers by the gate? You ought to know better than to bring children to the pond. After all the trouble I've gone to trying to keep them out. A child almost drowned in here last winter, when the pond was frozen over.'

'Perhaps you should lock the gate,' Helen said firmly, and her quiet tone halted his tirade and caused him to look at her keenly.

'You're a stranger in these parts, aren't you? I haven't seen you before.'

'I'm Helen Barclay, the new district nurse.' Helen explained what had happened, and saw the anger seeping out of the man's face.

'Sorry, Nurse,' he said, smiling thinly. 'I'm Russell Thorpe, of Thorpe's Farm. This is my land, and I've been trying to keep the local children away from this pond ever since I've been here. Young

Tommy Brace's father works for me. This young fellow is a regular terror. He comes here to the pond, leaves my gates open, and chases the animals and the fowls whenever he can get near to them. He made a bad mistake last year. I put a bull into this meadow in an attempt to keep the kids out, and Tommy came in to chase him. But you know the difference now between a bull and a cow, eh, Tommy?'

'Yes, Mr Thorpe. I promise I won't come here again if you don't tell my dad!'

'I'll tell him all right!' Russell Thorpe threatened, but he smiled at Helen, and his face seemed more attractive without the forbidding expression he had worn when he came up.

'I'll see the children home and have a word with their parents,' Helen said.

'It will need more than that to scare them. If I lock the gate they make holes in the hedge. I don't know what to do. It's a real problem, and there's a great danger here for children. They skate here when the pond is frozen, and swim during the summer. One of these days someone will get drowned.'

'Have you ever thought of filling it in?' Helen enquired. She looked past him at the meadow. 'There's a great mound over there that spoils the look of the field. A bulldozer would push it into the pond in a matter of an hour or so.'

'You're a drastic person,' he said, smiling as he turned to survey the meadow. 'It's a neat solution, but what about my cattle? They drink from this pond.'

'Two or three troughs up near your house would be easy to fill from your own water supply, surely!' Helen was serious as she considered the problem. 'Surely a little expense is worthwhile in averting such a terrible danger to the local children. I'm sure you would never forgive yourself if one of the children happened to meet with an accident here. It's all very well putting up warning notices, but these children aren't old enough to understand.'

He was nodding all the time she spoke, and there was a faint smile on his thin lips. Helen could not help noticing that his biceps bulged under his rolled up sleeves, and she had never seen a wider pair of shoulders. His face was very weathered and brown, and he looked the picture of health. She wouldn't be seeing him in any professional capacity, she thought remotely.

'I presume you're a very good nurse,' he said. 'I hope you will like Bullingham. I settled here some years ago, and I've never regretted it.'

'Thank you, Mr Thorpe,' Helen replied. 'Now I shall take the children home.'

'They live just along there,' he informed her. 'There are a dozen council houses. My father was a fool to sell that piece of land to the Council.'

Helen smiled as she led the children away, and he came with them as far as the gate, opening it to let them through, and he warned Tommy Brace again to stay away from the pond. But his anger had gone, and Helen went on with the children. When she glanced back she saw that Russell Thorpe was still standing at the gate watching her.

He was a nice man, she thought as they entered a narrow road that led to the small cluster of houses. The children began to get restless, and Tommy suddenly darted ahead and sped in through the nearest gateway. Two women stood at the gate, talking, and they turned to study Helen as she approached with the girls.

'Good evening,' Helen said in friendly tones. She surveyed the tall, thin woman standing in the gateway as if she lived there. 'Are you Tommy's mother?'

'I'm Mrs Brace.' There was some suspicion in the voice, and the pale eyes watched Helen carefully.

'I'm Helen Barclay, the new district nurse.' Helen went on to tell them how she had met the children. She saw the suspicion fade a little from the watchful eyes, and the other woman bent to take up Mary James in her arms.

'Mary, haven't I told you not to go near that pond?' she demanded in shrill tones. She was young, not more than twenty-five, Helen judged, but she was untidily dressed, and pregnant, Helen noticed. 'Thank you, Nurse, for taking the trouble to fetch them away. The little devils; they're always playing over there. It's about time Farmer Thorpe did something about that pond.'

'It's no good talking to the children, Nurse,' said Mrs Brace. 'They're not old enough to understand. It's only natural for the children to go where there's water.'

'It will be a tragedy if anything happens to one of them,' Helen said. 'I'd take more steps about the matter if I had a child here.'

'Do you like Bullingham?' Mrs Brace demanded.

'I think I shall.' Helen nodded with certainty.

'It's all right in the summertime, but wait until you get called out in the middle of the night in the heart of winter.' Mrs James smiled widely. 'You'll be coming to see me in a few months, Nurse.'

'I'll be coming to see you before then,' Helen replied. 'I have all the notes that Nurse Griffin made on her cases, and I'll get around shortly to see everyone on the list.

'Nurse Griffin was around today,' Mrs Brace observed. 'I saw her going into Mrs Lark's. When will you start the rounds, Nurse?'

'Tomorrow. Nurse Griffin finishes her duties today.'

'It'll be better to have a younger nurse around,' Mrs James observed. 'Nurse Griffin has been past it for a long time.'

'We all have to get old,' Mrs Brace pointed out.

Helen smiled and took her leave of them, and she was aware of being under close scrutiny as she departed. She walked along the road until she came to the commercial centre of the village; a Co-op shop that sold everything in the groceries and vegetables line and had a small corner of its space made over into a post office, and a butcher shop that also sold fish. But Helen was interested only in the telephone, and she breathed deeply as she entered the kiosk to put through a call to the telephone engineering department.

The telephone, a most vital link between the nurse and her patients and the doctor, had been cut off when Nurse Griffin moved out of the bungalow to make way for Helen and her mother. It had been promised by the telephone people that the service would be reconnected immediately, but Helen was on the eve of commencing her duties with her line still out of action.

She made her call, and as it was evening the stand-by engineer was too busy to be reached. Helen left a message with the operator, impressing upon her the urgency of the matter, but she had a feeling that she would be without telephonic contact when her duties began. There were other calls to be made, both personal and in the line of duty, and afterwards Helen felt easy in her mind as she started back to the bungalow. She was enjoying the walk because all of this was strange to her, but with a wide country area to cover, encompassing several villages, she would use her small Triumph Herald when making her rounds.

The sound of a motor scooter behind her made her look around, and she saw a uniformed policeman bearing down on her. He slowed when he saw her, and she paused when he pulled up. She pushed her blonde curls out of her eyes, smiling as he greeted her.

'You must be Nurse Barclay,' he said, his keen brown eyes studying her closely. 'I'm John Godfrey, the local policeman. 'I'm pleased to meet you, Nurse. I expect we'll be meeting quite a lot on the roads in future.'

'I'm sure we shall, constable,' Helen replied. 'I'll look out for you, especially at night. I expect a friendly face on a deserted road makes all the difference.'

'You won't meet many people abroad, and that's a fact,' he replied, speaking with a slight burr in his tones. He was not an old man, but Helen couldn't place his age with any accuracy. He might be anywhere in the thirty-to-forty age range. 'If you ever have any problems that might come within my scope then don't hesitate to let me know.'

'Thank you, constable, I'll remember that,' Helen told him. They walked on together, talking generally about the district, and when they reached her gate Helen paused.

'Nurse Griffin was a familiar sight around here for a good many years,' he told her as he prepared to depart. 'But she got too old for the job in the last few months. I hope you'll settle down nicely, Nurse. We need someone around here to take care of things.'

There was a warm feeling inside Helen as she watched him go on his way. It was nice to know that her services were really needed here. A lot of people would be relying on her in any emergency. These isolated areas were behind the times in lots of ways, of necessity because of location and distance from modern amenities, but she would be on hand, and no doubt once she settled into her new job she would begin to take up threads of living and start setting down roots.

Her mother opened the door to her, and Mrs Barclay was tall and slim, her hair still silvery blonde at the age of fifty-one, and she looked a good ten years younger. It was easy to see these were mother and daughter.

'Everything all right, dear?' Mrs Barclay demanded. 'Did you get through to the telephone people?'

'Yes, Mother. The operator will pass on a message. I expect we'll be connected first thing in the morning. We must be ready for some problems. I think we've done very well so far, don't you?'

'Very well.' Mrs Barclay led the way into the lounge. 'I've got everything straight now. You wouldn't think we'd just moved all the way from London.'

'Do you think you'll enjoy living here, Mother?' There was a spasm of uncertainty in Helen as she sat down on the sofa and studied Mrs Barclay's smooth face.

'I'm sure of it, Helen. Don't worry yourself about that, dear. You know I've always talked of having a nice home in the country. Town life lost its interest for me when your father died.'

'I know, Mother, but you're apt to get very lonely stuck here while I'm busy on my rounds. I'll be out most of the day, you know, and probably half the night sometimes.'

'I can always go with you for a change, Helen, and no doubt I shall find plenty in the garden and around the place to interest me Nurse Griffin has kept everything very well.'

'She told me there was an old-age pensioner who comes several times a week to do most of the garden for her,' Helen said. 'I expect he'll come and give us a look before long. We'll keep him busy, shall we? No doubt he looks forward to the few shillings he earns.'

'I'll join the Women's Institute,' Mrs Barclay said. 'In a few months I shall be converted to country life. You won't know that I haven't lived here all my life.'

'That's the only thing I shall worry about,' Helen admitted.

'Don't worry about me, my dear,' her mother replied gently. 'But what about you? It really isn't right for a girl of twenty-seven to bury herself out here in the wilds of Norfolk.'

'I have my work,' Helen pointed out. 'That's all I need.'

'Perhaps, but only time will tell. You will persist in your assertions that you were not deeply in love with Harold, but I can't help feeling that your manner suggests that your emotions were more deeply stirred. Perhaps you don't realize it yourself, Helen, but you've been very restless these past few weeks. I only hope we have taken the right step, because if we haven't then we're in for a lot of unhappiness.'

'We can always move on after a year or two,' Helen said cheerfully. 'Don't worry about it, Mother.'

'The optimism of youth,' Mrs Barclay said softly. 'But I can't exactly call you youthful, Helen. You're an adult, and have been for quite a number of years. It sometimes surprises me just how the time has flown. It seems only a short while ago that you were a girl at school.'

'Would you like to go out for a drive, Mother?' Helen asked. 'You've been extremely busy settling in. I think we could both do with a change of atmosphere. Tomorrow I start work. I shall have to drop in to Doctor Arden's office from time to time to check with his secretary. But it will be a succession of long days and nights, from what I've learned. We won't have much time for one another after today.'

'It doesn't matter, so long as you're happy, Helen,' Mrs Barclay replied wisely . . .

They went for a drive that evening,

and afterwards Helen went to bed. She lay for a long time just thinking about the past, present and future, and of the three the past was heaviest in her mind. But she was concerned only with the future, for now the present would take care of itself.

Next morning she was awake early and ready to leave on her first round. With a good breakfast inside her and her case packed, with her list of patients well checked and with her, she went out to the dark green car and started away from the bungalow, waving to her mother as she departed. She had an itinerary worked out, and felt happy and joyful as she drove through the bright morning sunshine.

Her first call was in the village, and she attended to Mrs Bartram, an old lady of eighty-four whose eyes were giving her trouble. But she had to answer questions about herself, and was no less slow in asking background questions about her patient, a practice she was to follow for the rest of the day.

She found her older patients apt to be slow in accepting her in place of the older woman they had known so very long, but Helen was well trained and knew how to cope with all types. A ready smile and a few comforting words were all that were necessary to win over the majority of cases.

By the time she had finished her morning round Helen was four miles from home, having travelled in a wide half-circle, but she was well up with her work, and went back to the bungalow for lunch. Mrs Barclay was looking for her when she arrived at *Wistaria*, and Helen parked the car and went thankfully into the bungalow.

'What kind of a morning has it been, Helen?' Mrs Barclay demanded.

'It went very smoothly, but I've still got a lot of ground to cover,' Helen replied. 'What about the telephone?'

'An engineer came this morning and connected us. So don't forget to ring me during your rounds in future, in case I have anything to report.'

'I'll remember,' Helen promised.

'Doctor Arden called just after eleven,' Mrs Barclay said.

'On the telephone?'

'No, in person. He was doing his round. He is a nice old gentleman. He told me he's taking on a younger partner. He and Nurse Griffin always had a standing joke that when one of them retired the other would soon follow. He told me he's been taking care of the health of the people in this area for more than thirty years!'

'I like him,' Helen said, 'and I'll miss him if he retires.'

'It won't be long before he does leave, because his new partner starts next week.'

'So there's a clean sweep right through the medical world in this area,' Helen said. 'They say new brooms sweep clean, so we'll all have to be on our toes for some time to come.'

'No-one will ever be able to fault your work,' Mrs Barclay said, smiling.

'I certainly hope I don't give anyone

cause to complain,' Helen replied. 'Now I'd better have lunch, Mother, and be on my way again. I've got an expectant mother to see this afternoon in the village of Hansford, and her time is getting short. We can expect the happy event within the next week, so the reports inform me.'

'That's wonderful, Helen. It will be nice to know that your own first maternity case will be behind you. Don't you feel worried about anything that faces you in your job?'

'Nothing worries me in my department,' Helen replied seriously. 'I've had a good training, and qualified really well in everything that matters. I may not look it to my new patients, but I have more qualifications than Nurse Griffin, and more up to date ideas.'

'And that is everything,' Mrs Barclay said with confidence in her tones. 'I do believe you've already settled down in happy optimism, Helen, and I hope it will last.'

2

Helen felt that she had settled down when the first week was behind her. She knew she was becoming a familiar sight driving around the district in her little car, and most people now paused to look and wave as she went by. Her patients, mostly ageing people unable to get to the doctor's surgery and not ill enough to be sent into the hospital at Norwich, soon came to accept her. Word began to spread about her efficiency and cheerfulness. When she attended Mrs Jerrow in confinement and safely delivered an eight-pounds boy her own happiness matched that of the mother. As she was finishing off her work after the confinement she heard a car pulling up outside, and Mr Jerrow went in answer to admit the doctor. Helen found herself staring into the cool grey eyes of a young stranger, who quickly introduced himself as Martin Reade, Dr Arden's new partner.

'I'm very pleased to meet you, Nurse Barclay,' he said quickly. 'You've only just taken up your appointment here, haven't you? How do you like it? I've been hearing all about you from some of the patients.'

'I'm very happy here, and I hope you will be, too,' Helen replied. 'I had heard you were coming.'

'This is my first day,' he admitted. 'It seems so leisurely after working in a hospital. But how's Mrs Jerrow? I understand there's nothing for me to do. I came as soon as Mr Jerrow called.'

'Everything is under control, Doctor,' Helen said. 'Come and see young master Jerrow.'

Martin Reade didn't stay long, and after he had gone Helen took her leave, happy in the knowledge that she had left two very relieved and happy people behind. She was smiling gently to herself as she drove home, thankful that she hadn't been called out in the middle of the night, and the evening was still young as she went back to Bullingham. But she stopped in the village of Actford to telephone her mother, and learned that no other calls had come in during her absence. She informed Mrs Barclay that she was on her way home, and imparted the news of the Jerrow baby. As she left the kiosk a large car drew up beside her.

'Good evening, Nurse Barclay,' the driver called, and Helen recognized Russell Thorpe.

'Hello, Mr Thorpe, she replied. 'Have you done anything about that pond yet?'

'Not yet. We aren't all made of the same mould, Nurse. I understand you're doing a good job in the district. I haven't had a chance to see you again, but when do you get off duty? If you have no objections I'd like to have your company on some bright evening.'

'Thank you, but I'm far too busy to have any free time,' Helen replied, shaking her head.

'I suppose there's someone else in your life,' he remarked sorrowfully. 'A beautiful girl like you can't have escaped the pack.'

'You put it so beautifully,' she retorted. 'You're not exactly forbidding yourself. How have you managed to avoid being trapped?'

'I can see that you're a girl who gives as good as she gets,' he said with a shake of his head. 'But no-one ever tried to trap me. I was always too busy in those early, formative years. Now I've settled down into farming and I don't get the opportunities that seem to be the prerogative of youth. However you seem to be exactly what I've been looking for half my life, so if you do get an evening free now and again why don't you give me the pleasure of your company?'

'I get so little free time that when I am off duty I like to take my mother out, because she's always in the house.'

'Then would you and your mother care to join me for tea one Sunday afternoon? I'm sure you must be interested in farming, and I'd enjoy showing you over my place. Both my parents are dead now, but I have a housekeeper who makes wonderful scones. You really ought to try them.'

'Thank you, you're very kind.' Helen smiled. 'I'm sure Mother would like to avail herself of your offer.'

'Then I may expect you this Sunday afternoon?' he demanded eagerly. 'I'll come and pick you up if you wish.'

'I'm afraid I always have to use my own car in case I get called out,' she replied. 'We'll drive over, and I shall look forward to seeing your farm.'

'I'll expect you about three, shall I?' He was smiling, his dark eyes filled with pleasure. 'I spend such lonely Sundays,' he confided. 'You wouldn't believe the half of it.'

Helen found her thoughts in a whirl after they had taken leave of one another, and as she drove homeward she had to compel herself to concentrate upon her driving. Russell Thorpe had an overpowering personality, and she could remember his bright smile and dark, intense eyes as if he were still before her.

Mrs Barclay was thrilled when Helen told her of the invitation, and it was agreed that they would accept.

'But you're not the only one to collect an invitation, Helen. The vicar called while you were out, and he wants to meet you. He also extended an invitation for the both of us to visit the vicarage. He's only a young man, not quite what you'd expect in a vicar, but very nice. I told him we'd be glad to accept, but that your work governed everything in this house, and he said he'd see us again to talk to you.'

'So we're being accepted, Mother,' Helen said lightly. 'I can hear some of my friends talking now. You'll have to live in the village for twenty years before the locals will even speak to you, they said. You'll regret the day you moved out of Town!'

'Well you don't, do you?' Mrs Barclay demanded.

'Not a bit of it. I've never felt better either physically or mentally. What about you?'

'I'm thoroughly enjoying myself. The garden keeps me busy, and the neighbours are already beginning to show their faces. I've been asked to join the Women's Institute, and I think that will devour any free time I may have. But we do have the winter to face, Helen!' A trace of anxiety made itself present in Mrs Barclay's tones. 'Do you think you'll be able to cope with the weather then?'

'Nurse Griffin did for more than twenty-five years! I'm sure I can do as well!'

'That's the spirit.' There was a warm note in Mrs Barclay's voice. 'In six months, when the bad weather does start, we'll both be really rural.'

'You mean I'll be going out on my rounds with a straw in my mouth or a piece of grass between my front teeth,' Helen said with a laugh.

'I don't think we'll get as bad as that,

but it's all a matter of attitudes. Now that we're into our second week I don't mind telling you I was worried about the change, although I wouldn't mention it before. But now we seem to be settling in quite nicely I can talk about it. You're sure you're not missing the bright lights, Helen?'

'Not a bit of it! You seem to forget that I didn't see much of the bright lights anyway. In nursing there's either very little time or money for that sort of thing. I feel more satisfied here, Mother, as if this part of nursing is my true vocation.'

The doorbell rang, and Mrs Barclay went to answer. Helen wondered if it was another call for her, but she didn't mind. She felt as if she wanted to be on the go all the time, and could not help thinking that perhaps the past, the unfortunate business of Harold, was still niggling subconsciously in her mind. But Mrs Barclay came back with a smile upon her face.

'It's Doctor Reade, Helen. He'd like

to talk to you. I've shown him into the lounge. He's as nice as you say he is.'

Helen nodded and went to the lounge, where she found Dr Reade standing at the window and staring out at the garden. He turned at her entrance, and smiled at her, dressed casually in flannels and sports jacket, with a white open-necked shirt underneath.

'Good evening, Nurse Barclay,' he greeted. 'I hope I'm not disturbing you. But I have the list of patients for you to visit. I know it's usually telephoned through to you, but as I had nothing to do this evening, and being off duty, I thought I'd bring it along myself.'

'That's very kind of you, Doctor,' Helen said with a smile. 'It is a beautiful evening, isn't it?' She took the sheet of paper which he held out to her. 'What do you think of Truston?'

'It's a quaint little place, and very quiet, which is just how I like it. I understand you've only just taken over this district, and that you come from

London. How are you settling in?'

'Very well, thanks. Mother and I were just talking about it. We've both taken to the country. I thought I would, but I was worried about Mother, and she thought she would but was worried about me. Are you used to the country, Doctor?'

'As a boy,' he replied. 'I was brought up in the country in a village about ten miles from here. I've never forgotten it. I have been working in a hospital in Birmingham, but I've always wanted to go into private practice, and now the opportunity has arrived.'

'Of course, this is your first day, isn't it?'

'That's right, and I thought I'd take a look around and familiarize myself with the district we cover. It wouldn't do to get called out in the middle of the night and not know where to go.'

'Are you managing to find your way around?' Helen demanded.

'It's a bit difficult,' he admitted. 'I can find the villages all right, but some of the houses are scattered, and all lanes look alike. They don't make a practice of putting the names of lanes up, do they?'

'No. I was lucky in that Nurse Griffin, my predecessor, was here long enough to show me around. But I'm not doing anything this evening, beyond standing by and if you wouldn't mind my company then I'll be only too pleased to go with you and show you around.'

'Would you be so kind?' He smiled, and his brown eyes were filled with brightness. 'The reason I brought that list was in the hope that I could get you to offer your help. But I do feel guilty about it because I know your time is very limited.'

'I don't mind,' Helen said. 'I'll just tell Mother where I'm going, and the route we'll take. Then I can ring her at intervals to see if I'm needed anywhere. I'll take my case with me, just in case.'

'That's a good idea. I've got my bag in the car. If you are needed then the patient will get a shock to see the both of us turning up.'

'Excuse me a moment,' Helen said with a smile. 'I'll change out of uniform. I don't suppose I'll be called, although I do have two maternity cases getting near to the end of their time.'

She left the lounge and hurried to find her mother, who smiled warmly at the news.

'I'm glad for your sake, Helen,' Mrs Barclay said. 'You do need some relaxation, you know. And I think he's a very nice person. Enjoy yourself, dear, and I'll take any messages that may come through.'

'I'll ring you from each of the villages,' Helen promised. 'We won't be long, I don't suppose. I can understand the difficulties because I felt so strange despite having been shown around by Nurse Griffin.'

She went to change her uniform for a biscuit coloured dress that had a high neck and was sleeveless, and a comb through her blonde curls was all that she needed for her short style. Taking a pink cardigan with her, she presented herself to Martin Reade, and saw approval in his dark eyes.

'I wouldn't have known you out of uniform, Nurse,' he said slowly.

'I'm very rarely out of uniform,' she replied.

Mrs Barclay saw them off, and Helen could not help a sigh of relief as she sat in the big black car beside him and they went off along the lane.

'This is a treat,' Helen said. 'It's strange sitting in a car and not being the driver.'

'I saw your Herald,' he replied. 'A nice little car. But you can relax now. You're not driving it.'

Helen smiled, and settled back to look around at the countryside.

'This is the first time I've been able to see beyond the roadside,' she said. 'That's the worst of driving a car. One's mind can never get beyond the verges.'

'That's true.' He glanced at her. 'This is very lovely country, you know.'

'I've found that out already. But you say you were brought up in this area.' She glanced at him, and caught her breath as realization came to her. 'Oh!' she said.

'What's wrong?' he demanded.

'If you were brought up in this district then you don't need to be shown around the villages, do you? I expect you know them better than I.'

He smiled broadly. 'You're very perceptive. It didn't take you long to see through my subterfuge. I must confess now that I used my strangeness here to get you out with me. But I had nothing to do this evening, and I imagined that you didn't go far in the evenings. I'm a stranger here and so are you. I didn't think you had made friends yet with anyone.'

'I see.' She nodded. 'You've been very thoughtful, Doctor. But I must confess that I'm enjoying myself.'

'Well that makes it all right,' he commented. 'If we're each going to be in our respective jobs only half as long as our predecessors then we shall become very good and long established friends, so we may as well break the ice as soon as possible.'

'I have no immediate plans for moving on anywhere,' Helen said.

'And neither have I.' He sighed. 'I had a bit of a nerve for intruding upon you as I did, but when I met you this morning I had the feeling that you were the type of girl I ought to make friends with. It can be very lonely out here in the country, and it wouldn't do you any good to be on duty twenty-four hours of the day with no relaxation.'

'You're the doctor,' Helen said brightly, and she was feeling light-hearted as she spoke.

'My name is Martin,' he retorted.

'And I'm Helen.'

'Good. I'm glad I've cleared the air a bit, Helen. Now let's enjoy a nice drive, shall we?'

'I'm looking forward to every minute of it,' she replied with a gay laugh.

By the time the evening came to an

end they were feeling very friendly. Helen felt a little sad as they drove back to Bullingham. But she was uplifted by happy feelings that would not leave her. Martin was a first-class companion, and very cheerful. They had joked and chatted through two and a half hours, and when he brought the car to a standstill outside the bungalow Helen felt as if they were old friends.

'Thank you for such a nice evening, Martin,' she said.

'It was my pleasure entirely,' he replied. 'I hope we'll be able to get together again, Helen. I get two or three evenings off a week, and perhaps we can arrange to go out again.'

'I'd love to,' she replied.

'Then I'll give you a ring the next time I'm free. But I expect we'll be seeing each other on our rounds. I shall keep my eyes open for you. I did give you that list of new patients you have to visit, didn't I?'

'Yes, before we came out,' she replied. She was reluctant to get out of the car, but he had seven miles to drive into Truston. 'Thank you again, Martin.'

'I'll be seeing you,' he replied with a smile, and she alighted. He lifted a cheery hand to her as he drove off, and Helen stood in the soft gloom and watched him out of sight.

She sighed heavily when he had gone, and shook her head slightly as she considered him. It was kind and thoughtful of him, she told herself, and felt heat come into her cheeks when she thought of the method he had used to get her into his car. He had come to visit her just for that very reason, and she was glad. He was very nice, and seemed just the type for her to know. He had said the same about her! Helen was thoughtful as she walked up to the bungalow, and she paused for some moments to compose herself before going in to face her mother.

Mrs Barclay was preparing supper when Helen went into the kitchen, and before speaking she studied Helen's face intently.

'No need to ask if you've had a nice time, dear,' she commented. 'I'm so happy Dr Reade came along. He's young, and he's very nice. It would be wonderful if you and he became close friends. You need someone like him, Helen, to help you along.'

'He's extremely nice,' Helen said softly. 'I really like him, Mother. It was a treat to meet someone like him.'

'Good.' Mrs Barclay nodded vigorously. 'With Dr Reade and Farmer Thorpe, as they call him around here, you won't lack the kind of company you need, Helen.'

'I can see the trend of your thoughts, Mother,' Helen accused with a laugh. 'But I'm going to be much too busy to bother with that sort of thing. After Harold I vowed I'd never look at another doctor again, so that lets Martin out. And I must say that Russell Thorpe looks like a confirmed bachelor to me.'

'That's why he's asked us to tea on Sunday,' Mrs Barclay said shrewdly. 'All right, Helen, you think what you like, but I know different.'

Helen made no reply to that, and after they had eaten supper she felt tired enough to welcome her bed. But it seemed she had hardly closed her eyes before the telephone rang, and she went quickly in answer. An agitated male voice spoke excitedly in her ear.

'Nurse Barclay! This is Mr Betts.'

'Yes, Mr Betts.' Helen knew he was one of the two expectant fathers she had shortly to contend with.

'It's my wife, Nurse. She's in pain, and I think her time has come.'

'Tell me about her pain. Is it regular? At what intervals?' Helen glanced at her watch. It was just after four a.m., and dawn was breaking the sky in places.

'She's been lying awake most of the night,' came the reply. 'She says the pains are getting worse.'

'Very well, I'll come at once. Don't worry, Mr Betts.'

'All right, Nurse. I'll be looking for you.' The relief that sounded in his tones compensated Helen for the early hour.

She went to get dressed, and left the bungalow quietly, not wishing to waken her mother, but the sound of the car's engine was like the starting motors of a moon rocket leaving the launch-pad. Helen thinned her lips as she drove down the lane. She hadn't far to go, and she stifled a yawn as she watched the road in the headlights. A rat scuttled into the grass by the verge, and she shuddered. If there was one thing she didn't like it was the rat family.

The village was still dark and silent as she drove through it, and when she came to the Betts' house, standing in solitary vigil beside the main road, she saw a light in an upper and a lower window. Before she was out of the car Mr Betts, a youngish man who worked on a farm, was waiting at the door for her.

'Good morning, Mr Betts,' Helen said briskly. 'How is your wife?'

'In pain,' he replied worriedly. 'I'm so

glad you're here, Nurse.'

'There's nothing to worry about,' Helen said with a smile. They went into the house, and she went up to the bedroom to see Mrs Betts. The woman was tight-lipped and apprehensive. She stared at Helen as if she were some sort of ogre.

'I hope we haven't got you out on a wild-goose chase, Nurse,' she said worriedly. 'It's so early. I've been hanging on half the night because I didn't want to have you answering a false alarm.'

'You don't have to worry about that,' Helen said cheerfully. 'I'd rather be called too early than too late, you know. Now let's have a look at you.'

'I kept poor Ron awake, too,' the woman said. 'I wish it was all over.'

'It will be some time today,' Helen announced, after making an examination. 'But not to worry yet. Let's time your pains, and then you can have a nice cup of tea.'

'You're such a comfort,' Mrs Betts

told her in little more than a whisper. 'I was afraid, but now you're here it's all right.'

'That's the spirit. There's nothing to be afraid of. Everything will be all right, and by this time tomorrow that cot in the corner will have its little occupant.' Helen smiled reassuringly. 'I'll leave you now, but I'll be back at nine, before I start my round. Your mother will be with you during the day, I think you said.'

'That's right, Nurse. Ron goes to work early, but Mother comes in early.'

'Good. You have nothing to worry about before I come again. I'll be in at nine, and then, if it isn't time, I'll see what's happening. Try and rest, won't you?'

'Yes, Nurse. Thank you for coming.'

'I'll have a word with your husband on my way out,' Helen said, and left the room. She found Ron Betts in the kitchen, and eased some of his anxiety with her confident words. When she took her leave she sighed deeply. The coming day would see the arrival of a new child into the world, and the fact that she would deliver it filled her with humility. She paused by her car to stare around into the gloom. The sky was breaking up now, and to the east there was a belt of definite light. Overhead the greyness was clawing through the blackness as the two extremes battled for possession of the sky.

Helen smiled gently to herself. These were moments when the whole job of nursing showed its compensations. The early hour and the fact that she had broken her sleep did not enter into it. The relief which husband and wife in the house behind her had shown at sight of her more than compensated But it was the knowledge that her life was worthwhile, that the service she was able to supply made her necessary and justified her existence that counted with her, and she went home to resume her rest until morning came or the next call interrupted her life. She felt strangely contented as she drove back to the bungalow. Life was beginning to show promise again after her recent disillusionment, and she knew now without doubt that taking this position as District Nurse was the right decision. She was already feeling a sense of belonging to this community . . .

3

Young Andrew Betts was born that day just after two in the afternoon, and after the delivery Helen telephoned Doctor Arden and reported it before going on with her round. She was behind time due to the confinement, and had several patients to see. There was tiredness in her as she went on, but she was happy. She seemed to be getting into the swing of things now. The people were beginning to accept her, and with two successful maternity cases to her credit some of the suspicion she knew existed because she seemed so young was dying. She felt well pleased with herself as the day progressed.

Her life was settling into definite patterns, and she found herself busy from morning till night, covering a great deal of ground to get her work done. But this was a less restricted life and compared favourably with the job of general nursing which she had left. Her freedom here was in the distance she travelled and the different cases she was called upon to attend. She was her own boss in the handling of the patients, so long as the doctor's instructions were obeyed.

But she was tired in the evenings, for the fresh air took its toll of her vitality, apart from the longer hours she worked. In a hospital a nurse had her shift to work, and beyond that was rarely called in to perform extra duties, but a district nurse was always at the beck and call of the patients. A seriously ill person would be visited by the doctor once or twice a day, and the nurse might have to go as many times to give injections or the like. A district nurse was an extension of the doctor's service, saving him the extra visits and the treatments given in the home of the patients.

She saw little of Martin Reade during the days that followed, but she knew he was busy with the country round. But on the odd occasion when they met accidentally during their rounds they paused to chat, and in a surprisingly short time they were quite at ease and very friendly.

On the following Sunday afternoon Helen and her mother drove to Thorpe's Farm, and Helen wondered if Russell Thorpe had forgotten the invitation he had extended almost a week before. She hadn't set eyes on him since that evening meeting, and was wondering if she ought to have telephoned. But she parked the car in front of the large, red-brick farmhouse and she and her mother alighted. As they walked to the door of the house it was opened and Russell Thorpe himself appeared.

'Hello,' he greeted effusively, and shook hands with Mrs Barclay when Helen introduced them to each other. 'I was wondering if you had forgotten. I didn't get the chance to see you after last Monday evening. But here you are, and I've been looking forward to your visit. I can't wait to show you around, and I'm sure you'll enjoy the experience.' He smiled as he took Helen's arm. 'Come along into the house. It's rather large for one person, don't you think?'

'It must take a great deal of caring for,' Mrs Barclay said. 'We have only a bungalow, but it takes me most of my time to keep it spotless.'

'I have a very good housekeeper in Mrs Farrell,' he replied as he ushered them into the house. 'She has a woman who comes in twice a week to take care of the heavier work, but otherwise she looks after the place alone. She's been with us for almost a generation, it seems. She was here when I was born, and although she's in her seventies now she won't give way and take extra help.'

Russell Thorpe proved to be an able host, and he did not have to try and impress Helen. The old farmhouse had been extensively modernised inside, and the furnishings were tasteful, showing Helen something of the character of the man. His presence was indicated in many small ways in the house, and he had a strong and virile personality.

As they sat down to tea Helen could not help thinking of Martin, and she tried hard not to compare the two men. They were totally different in every way, apart from their physical beings, for both were tall and dark, but there all similarities ended. Martin was quiet but cheerful, and Russell was extroverted, at home when he was the centre of attraction.

'Mrs Farrell is famous for her scones,' Russell said, his bright brown eyes glinting as the housekeeper appeared to serve them. 'I'm going to engage a maid against her will to relieve some of the work pressures on her, and Im hoping she'll teach the newcomer how to make those wonderful scones.'

'There won't be another woman working in this house while I'm in charge, Mr Russell,' the old lady retorted, her blue eyes gleaming in her craggy face. She smiled sweetly at Helen. 'I mean hired help, of course. If Mr Russell ever married and the new mistress decided to run the house herself then she'd find me no obstruction. I've been waiting a long time to see Mrs Thorpe.'

'And you'll have a lot longer to wait, Mrs Farrell,' Russell said with a laugh. 'I have the feeling that I'm what they call a confirmed bachelor.'

'Until the right girl comes along,' the housekeeper said loudly. 'It will happen to you one day, you'll see.'

'I'm looking forward to it,' he replied, his bold eyes upon Helen. 'But let's have that tea you've been so busy preparing for the past three hours. I'm sure it will bear out the praise I've been giving you. We don't often have guests in the house, and I hope they'll come again.'

'If they do it won't be on account of my cooking but due to your personality,' came the wise retort, and Helen smiled as she met Mrs Farrell's gaze and saw the bright interest in the old lady's eyes.

The tea was perfect, and the buttered scones were indeed something to be praised. Mrs Farrell joined them at the table, for she had become part of the Thorpe family through her years of service, and she chatted quite happily through the meal. It transpired that she was a regular visitor to the Women's Institute during the good weather, and Mrs Barclay arranged to call and see her at least once a week at the farm. By the time the meal was over it was obvious that the two older women had taken a liking to one another.

'I'm sure you won't be interested in wandering around the farm, Mrs Barclay,' Russell said as they got up from the table. 'Helen has expressed a desire to look around, so if you'll excuse us while you're finishing your conversation with Mrs Farrell I'll take your daughter away.'

'Go and enjoy yourselves,' Mrs Barclay said, and Helen did not miss the significance of the gaze that followed them out.

'Usually I work on Sundays,' Russell told her. 'I help with the milking and do all the odds and ends that tend to be overlooked during the week. Then on top of that there's all the paperwork. That grows with each successive year.'

'You sound as if you're a great deal more busier than I am,' Helen retorted as they crossed a yard to the cowsheds.

'I expect I put in as many hours as you, per week,' he retorted. 'But you're looking well on it, Helen.'

She smiled at the use of her name, and was again reminded of Martin. His face flashed into her mind as she began to learn the mysteries of a farm.

The cowshed surprised her, for there was modernization at its latest in the milking machines that took up valuable space. Russell went on to talk of separators as he pointed to masses of pipes, and most of it sounded like a foreign language to Helen, but she was interested, and listened intently to everything he had to say. When they went on and came eventually to the hen batteries she expressed her feelings of the unnatural methods of egg production and Russell agreed with her.

'But having a few hens running around the yards and laying when they like isn't profitable,' he said. 'A farmer is like any other businessman, Helen. He has to show a profit, and this is the only way to do it with hens.'

The farm was large, with many barns and outbuildings, and Helen was surprised and pleased to see several horses in a meadow, two of them with young foals trotting at their sides.

'I thought horses went out,' she observed.

'This is one of the rules I break deliberately,' he replied. 'There's always been a horse or two on the farm, and I can't break with tradition. Can you ride?'

'No, and I feel I might be afraid to try,' Helen replied, watching the magnificent animals.

‘Horses won’t hurt you,’ he retorted, smiling broadly. ‘I think I could make a country girl out of you, Helen. Come and meet the horses.’

They walked to a gate and stood silent for a few moments, under the watchful eyes of the animals. Then Russell called to them, and after some slight hesitation two of the animals came slowly towards the gate, followed by the foals and the others. Helen moved back a little as the animals reached the gate and stretched their necks to get a closer look at her.

‘All their thoughts are directed towards sugar or pieces of apple,’ Russell said, stroking the animals. ‘Come and make friends with them. They’re just like big dogs, Helen. They won’t hurt you.’

She went timidly to his side, and saw her reflection in the large brown eyes of the nearest animal. She lifted a hand slowly and patted a gleaming brown neck, and the horse snorted in some unintelligible language. Helen gained confidence, and when one of the foals came close and she held out a hand to it a small, velvety muzzle was thrust against her palm.

'Aren't they sweet?' she demanded, looking into Russell's face, and he nodded slowly, taking in the picture of her flushed and happy face and the sweet innocence of herself and the animal by her.

'Beautiful!' he announced. 'I've never seen a prettier picture. They've taken to you without hesitation. That tells me a lot about you, Helen.'

'Really?' she demanded.

'Of course. Next to the dog the horse is man's oldest friend, and you can't fool these animals. They know all about you in the first moment. It's a pity Man hasn't learned to sum up his fellow men, and women, as well, or only half as well. There wouldn't be half the trouble in the world.'

'You sound as if you've been crossed in love!' Helen watched his face for a moment, but he smiled as he shook his head.

'Not me. I've never been that serious about any girl. I've never met one yet who could attract me; present company excepted, of course.'

'Now you're showing your character,' she said with a laugh. 'Flatterer!'

'Compliments are cheap,' he said, laughing. 'Come on, and I'll show you the nearer parts of the farm. I own a tremendous acreage, something in the region of fifteen hundred. That's large around here.'

'However do you attend it all?' Helen demanded.

'Modern machinery,' he replied. 'Lately there's been a big trend to cutting down hedges and turning two or three small fields into one large one. That's mainly because smaller fields are no good for the modern, mechanical farmer.'

'Is it a good thing, losing the beauty of the countryside for the sake of more profit?' Helen shook her head slowly. 'One thing that makes Britain beautiful is the rows of hedges lining the roads and skirting the fields. The only thing I don't like about northern England are the stone walls.'

'I've already likened the farmer to any other businessman,' Russell said with a short laugh. 'There's been too much talk of the farmer relying upon hand-outs from the government. He's got to help himself, and taking down the hedges is only one small facet of the methods taken to improve yield and profit.'

'I always thought there was a great deal of romance in farming. But you make it sound too much like business.'

'You're learning,' he told her. 'There's hope for you yet, Helen.'

They walked along a path that wound around the edges of fields, and seemed to go on forever. As they walked Russell told her about the crops growing, pointing out fields of corn, each covered thickly with grass-like greenery, and fields of root crops, mainly sugar beet. Helen took it all in because it was new to her, and she didn't notice how time seemed to fly. When they reached some grazing land, where a great number of cattle gave Helen a perfect rustic picture, they paused and stood silent, listening to the natural sounds of the countryside. The evening was warm and pleasant, and sounds seemed to travel a great distance in the heavy solitude and silence. Behind them the roof of the farmhouse thrust up redly among a setting of green foliage, and the nearby church clock tolled the hour with echoing tones.

'How pleasant!' Helen felt touched by the grandeur of Nature. Not the slightest detail had been overlooked by some omniscient eye. Leaves were exquisitely formed on the branches, and the trees themselves were picturesque in their living mantles. Helen became aware of the smallness of herself compared to the universe and Creation. Life was a mystery from its source to the very end and afterwards, and she breathed deeply, trying to empty her mind of questions, wanting only to appreciate the beauty of it all without wondering about the whys and wherefores.

'I often come out here when I want to do some soul-searching,' Russell said gently, afraid to speak too loudly for fear of disturbing their mood. 'Standing here among all this peacefulness and solitude, one can't help wondering about the world and where its inhabitants are going? All the strife seems unimportant, insignificant, and quite useless. Far better to strive for the finer things, don't you think?'

'That's exactly what I feel,' Helen said slowly. 'Seeing this makes me believe that there is some great hand behind all the patterns. It can't come from Nature alone. There has to be some planned thought at the back of it.'

'I think in those terms myself.' His dark eyes seemed to glow as he stared into the reddening sun. There was a half smile upon his weathered face that gave Helen some indication of the peacefulness in his heart. He led a simple life, very close to Nature, and it showed in his ruggedly handsome face.

She felt a sudden stirring of emotion

inside her, and wondered at it. This experience was like drinking too much wine. It upset the senses, and the sudden glimpse beyond the rut of normal human life showed wider horizons than ever could be imagined. It was intoxicating, and to anyone unused to the sights and sensations it was overwhelming.

Russell suddenly put a hand upon her forearm, and Helen started as if he had slapped her. She looked up into his face, and saw the dark gleam of emotion in his eyes.

'I'm glad you've come to work among us, Helen,' he said softly. 'I can sense that you're all I ever thought I'd need in a woman, and there are no rivals in the background. You'll come to my house again, won't you?'

'Yes,' she replied without consideration. 'This is really beautiful, Russell. I think I can understand some of the feelings that flood the mind.'

'It doesn't happen to anyone,' he said sharply. 'Only a favoured few. I can remember walking one girl along here quite some years ago and all she could do was complain about the heat and the flies. It just goes to show, doesn't it?'

'It certainly does,' Helen said softly. 'So I pass the first of your tests, do I?'

'I'm not putting you through any kind of test!' he exclaimed.

'But you are,' she insisted with a laugh. 'I can tell that you're unconscious of the fact, but that's exactly what you are doing.'

'If I am then I'm sure you pass with flying colours,' he retorted. 'You're very perceptive, Helen. The more I see of you the better I like you.'

'I'm glad to know that,' she said dreamily.

'Are you?' He could not disguise the trace of eagerness that came with his words. 'You've made some sort of impact on me. I'll never forget that first evening I saw you. I took you for a trespasser.'

'Have you done anything about that pond yet, Russell?' she demanded, cutting across his words.

'No.' He shook his head. 'I haven't had time to think of it again.'

'You're a man with a great conscience,' she said keenly. 'I can tell that. If a child drowned in your pond it would have a terrible effect on your life. Don't leave it until it's too late, Russell, please.'

'I'll look into it, Helen,' he said quickly. 'I promise you. I like kids, so long as they stay away from the farm. You'd think country children would know better. A farm is a dangerous place for children, but they all think it's a playground.'

She nodded, aware of his presence now, her feelings stirred up by his words and the wonderful scenery about them. Spring, too, was having its subtle effect upon her. She could feel powerful emotions at work inside. She had never been one to show her feelings, but she had always been aware that deep and swift currents flowed through her. Now they bubbled close to the surface for the first time in many months. She trembled, becoming too aware of his presence. There was something about him that loosed romantic notions in her mind, and a tugging compulsion slowly made her realize that she wanted him to kiss her. He seemed to fit into this scene of things so well. He might have been a god of the earth come to adore her. She shivered as a tingling sensation travelled the length of her spine, and she found that he was still holding her arm.

Now he seemed only too aware of how she was feeling because he looked around to ensure they were alone before drawing her slowly into his embrace. Growing emotion seemed to blot out all else in Helen's mind. She breathed heavily as he took possession of her lips, and his arms were like steel bands around her waist and her shoulders. She closed her eyes and gave herself up for lost, knowing that all her recent resolutions about staying away from heartache and the men who caused it were dying quickly in the wave of feeling that surged through her.

The silence seemed to bind them more closely together than his embrace. A host of strange impressions chased themselves through her mind. Helen was aware only of his presence, and she didn't want him to stop kissing her. That was the most surprising thing about it. She had never been a flirt, didn't believe in casual romance, and yet she was urging this comparative stranger to kiss her, was holding him each time he drew back. But she was held herself firmly by a compulsion she could not understand, and when at last they drew apart they were both breathless.

'Well, he declared, staring into her eyes with a mesmeric intentness. 'I've kissed a few girls in my time, but nothing ever came from the contact. Now I've met you, and the impression I first got then has been strengthened. Helen, you've got to promise that you'll come to this very spot again.'

'Yes,' she said vibrantly, in tones that quivered. 'I can feel a kind of magic in the air.'

'That's not magic, it's a mixture of our presence, yours and mine,' he said. 'It doesn't happen very often, Helen, and we can't throw it all away as if it never happened. I knew the first moment I saw you that we could strike sparks together if we ever got the chance. Now I've been proved right.'

'Russell, I don't understand the half of what you're saying,' she said gently.

'But you can feel it in your heart,' he responded quickly. 'I can see it in your face. You know inwardly what I mean, don't you?'

'I think I do,' she conceded. 'You certainly know how to stir a girl's feelings.'

'That didn't come from experience,' he said with a trace of bitterness in his tones. 'It came straight from the heart of things. You and I are going to become very close friends, Helen, you mark my words.'

She sighed heavily and shook a little, and he put an arm around her waist and led her slowly back along the path. Helen felt as if she were enchanted, and intoxicated. There was a trembling weakness in her legs and a swirling of her senses inside her head. No man had ever affected her like that with a kiss. She felt as if the world had been turned upside down.

They were silent for most of the walk back to the house, and it seemed to Helen that the sights were clearer to her eyes and the sounds more keener. It was as if her senses had been brought into perfect focus for the first time in her life. Impressions were more brilliant and lasting, and she had the feeling that her life had been stepped up to a higher plane. Now she was really living, and all because of this strange man at her side. But he wasn't a stranger of only two weeks. He seemed to be the man she had been waiting for ever since she was old enough to dream.

But Russell seemed slightly ashamed

of the way his emotions had got out of hand, and he was silent, almost moody as they returned to the farmhouse. From time to time he glanced at her, and whenever their glances met he smiled gently. But Helen could see that he was concerned over something, and put it down to the fact that he felt he had been too bold on their first time together. The strange thing was that she disagreed with that thought. Any other man would have been thrust away before he could have kissed her, but with Russell she had sensed instinctively that it was different, and she had been powerless to stop him. In fact she had wanted him to do it, and that was the most amazing fact of all!

4

The evening passed so quickly that before Helen was able to recollect her scattered wits and start absorbing all the impressions she had gained it was time for them to return home. Russell made it plain he wanted to see Helen again, and insisted that she and her mother became regular visitors to the farmhouse. Helen agreed, and she knew by the tone in her mother's voice that she, too, had been favourably impressed. After taking their leave of Russell, Mrs Barclay couldn't talk enough about him on their drive home.

Helen listened to her mother's chatter with only half her concentration, for she was feeling the effects of that stroll with Russell through the fields. The man's personality had been overwhelming, and she could still feel a certain awe at the way he had aroused her from her slumbering state of emotions. There was a strange sensation of anticipation inside her, as if she were waiting for a storm to burst, and already her thoughts were turning to a state of wondering about Russell. Did he like her? Had he kissed her just because she was a woman and had been with him on a beautiful Spring evening? Or did it go any deeper than that? She had no way of knowing, but she realized with a start that she was quite prepared to have some more of the same treatment from him.

'You're not saying much, Helen,' Mrs Barclay said as they reached the bungalow. 'Didn't you take to him, dear?'

'I did,' Helen replied, stifling a sigh. 'I took a great liking to him. He was overwhelming, but very nice, and I shall look forward to seeing him again.'

'I'm so glad! We must take him up on his kind invitation to go again. I'm sure you and he could go very far together, Helen.'

'Now, Mother, don't get any ideas about match-making,' Helen warned with a laugh as she parked the car in the garage driveway. 'That sort of thing is best left to me.'

'I wouldn't dream of interfering to that extent,' her mother replied with a smile as they got out of the car. 'But I do wish you could meet a man who attracted you. I know you must be feeling that last incident very keenly. Harold didn't treat you right, dear, and another romance would take away the agony.'

'It wasn't like that, Mother. Harold never meant that much to me, I assure you. I'm not bitter or cynical about those matters, and I don't feel the slightest pang over parting with him.'

'Your work helps, no doubt. But you can't tell me that you were left untouched by it all.'

'I feel regretful at times.' Helen admitted that much. 'But even that is fading, Mother.'

They went into the house and Helen

slowly relaxed. The visit to Russell's had tensed her up considerably, she realized, and a shiver went through her when she recalled those sweet moments in his arms. She had never met a more forceful man, and yet he was very nice, and right and proper in his ways. It was a real pleasure to know him.

She went to bed that night with her mind filled with gentle impressions, and awoke in the morning feeling on top of the world. After breakfast she prepared a list of patients she had to visit, and as she was about to leave the house the telephone rang. She went in answer, and heard Russell's voice in her ear.

'How are you this morning?' he demanded. 'I trust you enjoyed yourself at mine yesterday?'

'More than you'll ever know,' she replied, feeling her pulses begin to race at the sound of his voice.

'All of it?' he asked. 'What about when we were alone in the fields?'

'Yes,' she replied gently. 'Even that. Thank you for being so kind, Russell.'

'It was my pleasure,' he replied. 'You don't mind me calling you at this time, do you?'

'Not at all, although I was on my way out to start my round. There's nothing wrong, is there?'

'Nothing that warrants your professional interest, but I'd like to take you out this evening, if it's at all possible.'

'I can't say yet, but you must understand that my work is very full-time,' she said regretfully.

'I could spend the evening with you at yours then,' he said eagerly. 'I couldn't care less what I do, so long as I'm in your company.'

'Then come round by all means! Mother and I will always be pleased to see you.'

'Your mother made a big impression on Mrs Farrell,' he went on, and laughed. 'Already she's asking when you're coming again, and that's what I'd like to know.'

'Perhaps you and Mrs Farrell would like to come here next Sunday,' Helen offered.

'We'll talk about it later in the week. You can expect me around this evening. What time, Helen?'

'Any time after seven,' she said. 'I usually finish rather late in the evenings, Russell.'

'All right. I must say I like the sound of my name on your lips, Helen. But I won't delay you any longer. I know you're a very busy girl. See you this evening. 'Bye for now.'

'Goodbye,' Helen replied, and held the phone to her breast for some moments after he had rung off. She stood lost in thought until her mother appeared to ask about the call. 'It was Russell,' she announced, and glanced at her watch. 'Good Lord! I must be on my way. If I get behind to start with I shall be lagging all day!'

'Mind the roads, dear,' Mrs Barclay called after her. 'Will you be home just after twelve for lunch?'

'I'll try,' Helen replied, leaving, and she hummed to herself as she drove along the lane.

It really was surprising how meeting a man could make a girl feel on top of the world! That fact was with her during the morning, and Helen could not control the waves of pleasurable anticipation that kept surging through her. She felt on edge, as if a long awaited treat was imminent. Her heart seemed to flutter and her hands trembled every time she thought of Russell. It was the strangest thing, the way he seemed to affect her!

Just before lunch Helen met Martin Reade, and they parked their cars in a nearby lay-by and Helen went across to him. He smiled happily when she got into his car beside him, and he opened his medical bag.

'I've got two more patients I want you to visit, Nurse,' he said. 'I've written down the details. I'd like you to see Mrs Lovell at around tea-time, if you can manage it. She's to have a second injection.' He handed her a slip of paper. 'All details are down there. But you'd better see if you can read my handwriting. Doctor's written word is always good for a joke, isn't it?'

'So they say.' Helen smiled as she scanned the paper. 'But I can understand this all right, Doctor. What about Mr Porter?'

'You can start calling on him tomorrow. I've attended to him today. Fit him into your regular list, will you?'

'Yes.' Helen nodded and folded the paper. 'It's a beautiful day, isn't it?'

'It is,' he agreed. 'I called at your home last night, but you were out.'

'I am sorry!' Helen stared at him, and there was a picture of Russell in her mind as she did so. She couldn't compare them! That was instantly obvious, and as she watched his gentle face she felt her sharp feelings for Russell waning inexorably. Recalling the evening she had spent with Martin Reade made her confused, for she liked him in a quiet, more determined way. Her feelings made that abundantly clear, even against her will. 'We went to tea at Thorpe's Farm,' she added slowly.

'Russell Thorpe,' he commented. 'Yes, I have met him. I hope you had a nice time.' He took a deep breath. 'Look, I was hoping to see you again this evening. I thoroughly enjoyed my evening out with you before, and we said we'd get together again. If you're not busy I'd like to call for you.'

'I'm afraid I shall be busy this evening,' she replied, looking him squarely in the eyes, and she saw disappointment fill him. A pang stabbed through her, and she wondered why she was feeling confused. Hadn't Russell proved yesterday that he was a man in a million when it came to interesting her? She recalled the exalted feeling which had gripped her ever since she awoke that morning. Now it was gone, and she was feeling tender towards this attractive man. Surely she wasn't turning into a flirt! The thought struck and made her feel guilty as he smiled.

'Well that's all right,' he said. 'Perhaps some other evening. I'm off duty every other night, so if you do get a free evening perhaps we can arrange something.'

'Of course,' Helen said slowly. 'I'd love to, Martin.' She spoke his name diffidently, aware that they were both on duty, but when she glanced at his face she saw he was smiling.

'I must be the shy type,' he admitted slowly. 'I don't seem to be able to find that nerve I had the other evening when I called for you at home.'

'Perhaps that only comes on during the evening,' she remarked.

'Well if it does I'll see you later,' he retorted lightly. Then he sighed. 'I'd like to take you for a drive around my own village, where I was born,' he went on. 'It's very beautiful, especially by the river. There's nothing more pleasant than to sit upon the bank in the cool of the evening. You strike me as being a girl who would like that sort of thing, and if you do then you wouldn't want to miss Halesby.'

'I've heard some of the patients talking about it,' Helen said. 'They all seem to think I ought to go there. We'll make a date to visit it, shall we?'

'What about Friday evening?' he queried.

'I'll make sure I'm free for it,' she replied.

'Good.' He reached out and touched her hand momentarily. 'Now I really must push on. I have so much to do. I'll look for you around the villages, Helen.'

'I expect we'll keep bumping into one another,' she replied, getting out of the car. ''Bye, Martin.'

'Cheerio,' he replied, and drove on.

Helen stood for a moment staring after his car, and a sigh gusted through her. What on earth was happening in her mind? Why had she suddenly wavered between Russell and Martin? Last night she had thought Russell the greatest thing ever to happen to her, and this morning when he had telephoned she thought she was walking on air. But seeing Martin had immediately returned her feet to the ground, and she could find no reason for her strange mental behaviour.

She went back to her car, still wondering, and as she went on, heading towards home for lunch, she tried to make some headway against her confusion. Was she really afraid, deep down inside, of falling in love with either Russell or Martin? Was that why her mind swung between the two, because she knew she couldn't love both men? She sighed. Perhaps she was trying to make too much of her meeting with them. She was still wary of men after her experiences with Harold, and now there were two men looming up in her mind and she could understand that it was only natural she would be afraid of committing herself one way or another.

When she reached home lunch was waiting for her, and she felt a little easier as she sat at the table with her mother. There had been no calls for her in her absence, but she still had a large list to contend with during the afternoon, and wanted to get on her way as soon as possible.

Mrs Barclay was still full of their previous day's outing, but although Helen arose to her mother's level she was feeling strangely empty inside, and knew it came from meeting with Martin that morning. But she dared not speak to her mother of it. No doubt Mrs Barclay would form her own opinions from that sort of confession, and Helen didn't want to be influenced in any way. She was relieved when it was time for her to go on with her work.

She found, upon visiting one of the farther villages in her district, that the third maternity case was due to be attended in the very near future, and made a note to be ready for any call. With two successful confinements behind her she was eagerly awaiting the third event. According to her notes there would be a gap of a month or two before the fourth case would arise.

But the afternoon passed quickly, with no problems to trouble her, and she bathed an old lady, treated an ageing farm-worker for leg ulcers, and gave injections to two other ladies. There were three young babies to attend, and two of them were suffering from measles. It was all a general day's work, and Helen was thoroughly satisfied with it as she finally turned homeward and considered that the bulk of the duties was over. If she didn't get any calls then she might be able to enjoy a quiet, restful evening. But a picture of Russell came to her mind, and she knew she would never be able to sit quietly with him. He was too alive and vibrant.

The feeling of confusion persisted in her mind as she went in to have tea with her mother. Afterwards she changed out of uniform and sat in the garden in a deck chair, lying back to absorb some of the sunshine. She was almost asleep when a Landrover pulled up at the gate, startling her with the roar of its powerful engine. Thinking it was a professional call, she sat up quickly, blinking her blue eyes, but it was a grinning Russell who came in at the gate.

'Hello,' he called. 'Hope I didn't

wake you. My car is out of action so I had to use the old Rover. How are you?'

'Fine thanks, if a little tired,' she replied. 'It's been a busy day. But I expect you've been a lot busier.'

'I don't work every day,' he replied. 'Today I had to go to market, and there's always enough paperwork to keep me chained to the desk for a couple of hours at a time.' He came close to her, staring down into her eyes, and Helen felt her pulses begin to race. She couldn't understand it because it had never happened to her before. It was as though his personality bludgeoned her own feelings out of existence and substituted only what he wanted her to feel. It was exciting and gratifying, but she knew it was like being lifted up on a merry-go-round. She would get dizzy before very long.

'I must be getting old,' she said with a smile. 'I'm beginning to feel the pace of my working day.'

'That's because you're never still,' he retorted, studying her keenly. 'You don't look a day over twenty-one.'

'Flatterer!'

'You called me that yesterday!' He walked with her under the shade of the trees flanking the garden, and paused to look around. 'It's very nice here,' he commented. 'Have you got everything you want?'

'In what way?' She watched him closely, her mind trying to repel his power. She tried to think of Martin, to keep his image in the background as a bulwark against this man's strange power. But it was like trying to stop a floodgate bursting, with only bare hands.

'In the gardening line! Nurse Griffin used to keep the place very well, but it's a bit old fashioned for a pleasant English garden.'

'I didn't know you had strong views on the matter.'

'I like rural England and all it stands for,' he said, dropping down on the grass and grinning up at her. 'Come and sit down,' he invited, and patted the warm ground at his side. Helen did so, but kept her distance. He was talking casually, but all the time she could sense his eyes upon her, devouring her, and she felt compelled to draw closer to him. He had a positively magnetic personality.

'I don't get much time for gardening,' she admitted. 'Mother handles that side of it. I help out whenever I have the time, which isn't very often. There is a pensioner who's arranged to come for two or three afternoons during the week. I believe Nurse Griffin had him to help her.'

'Im not very keen on gardening myself, but that's to be expected, having the farm to run.' He nodded soberly, his brown eyes glinting in the reddening sunlight. She heard him breathe deeply, and something like a sigh came from her. 'Of course the farmer's wife is supposed to feed the chickens and look after the gardens, but there's no wife at Thorpe's Farm.'

'Why not, Russell?' Helen asked. 'I

know what you told me, but perhaps you were just joking about not finding the right girl. There must have been times when you thought you had found the right one.'

'More than once,' he admitted. 'But I'm near to being a perfectionist, and I've never yet found a girl who could come close to my ideals.' He paused and smiled at her. 'Present company excepted, of course.'

Helen smiled. She liked watching the sun playing upon his weathered face. It gave him a rugged look, made him seem solid and dependable, but somewhere in the remoter parts of her mind she was beginning to hear warning bells sounding. It was strange after the way he had affected her the previous evening, and she wondered why Martin had been able to manage that effect upon her. Until she had met Martin that morning she had been all right.

Mrs Barclay appeared, and waved to Helen, who got to her feet with an apology coming to her lips. She excused herself and hurried towards her mother, aware that Russell was watching her slim figure with interest.

'Sorry to trouble you, Helen,' Mrs Barclay said, 'but there's a telephone call for you.'

'Is it Mrs Lovell?' Helen demanded.

'Your next maternity case?' Mrs Barclay shook her head. 'It's Doctor Reade.'

Helen nodded and went into the house, and her heart seemed to flutter a little as she took up the receiver. She drew a deep breath before speaking, and was a little surprised when her voice did sound completely natural.

'Hello, Martin,' she said.

'Helen! Get through your day all right?'

'Yes thank you. Is there anything wrong?'

'No. This is a social call. I know you said you couldn't get away tonight, but I thought I'd make a second try for you. Can you get away for an hour or so?'

'I don't think so, Martin.' She spoke

with true feelings of reluctance welling up inside her. It was on the tip of her tongue to tell him about Russell's presence, but somehow she didn't want him to know. She thought of Russell, sitting out there on the lawn, and could not fathom out her feelings. She wanted to see Martin as well. Both men were totally different in manner, like light and shade, and she was attracted to both. But perhaps there was safety in numbers. She was beginning to feel that she didn't want to get serious about either of them.

'Are you expecting to be called out?' Martin asked, breaking into her thoughts.

'Not really!' She was evasive because she didn't want to tell him the truth. That worried her because she didn't know why. Martin didn't mean anything to her, any more than Russell did, but she was becoming secretive. What did it mean?

'All right, Helen. I'll call you some other time. Sorry I disturbed you.'

'No, Martin, it's all right,' she replied

quickly, not wanting him to get the wrong idea. 'You're not disturbing me. Look, I'll go out with you the next time you're off duty in the evening. All right?'

'Yes, fine,' he said immediately. 'Thanks, Helen. I'll hang up now.'

'Goodnight, Martin,' she said, and lowered the receiver.

She found she was trembling, and frowned as she replaced the receiver. What was happening to her? It had started the previous evening when she had been with Russell alone in the fields. His kisses had set fire to her, caused a throbbing sensation in her heart that would not fade. But Martin had some influence upon her, and that was what was causing the confusion inside her. It was as if both men had invaded her mind with their different personalities and were fighting for the right to occupy the most prominent position. Helen sighed heavily as she went outside again, to find Russell upon his feet and talking animatedly with her mother.

'Have you got to go out, dear?' Mrs Barclay demanded.

'No. It was just another patient to be added to my list,' Helen lied, and compressed her lips as she considered the fact. She was turning into an inveterate liar. Whatever she had been in the past, demure, straightforward and quiet, she was now beginning to form all manner of nasty habits. But whose influence was doing this to her? Was it Russell or Martin at the back of it?

'It's going to take a lot of getting used to,' Russell said with a smile.

'What's that?' Helen demanded.

'Seeing you running off every so often to answer a call, and not knowing when you'll be coming back. Is a nurse's life always like that?'

'Usually, in this branch of the business,' Helen said with a smile. 'But I don't think I shall get called out tonight. There is a confinement due almost any day now, but I think I have a few days grace before the happy event.'

'Of course, you're the midwife, too, aren't you?' He nodded slowly. 'What a lot of studying you must have done in your youth, Helen.'

'That's the way it goes.' She suddenly felt old and worldly, and wondered if her life was following the pattern set out for her by her decision to become a nurse. Now she was living in a quiet backwater, and life might seem to pass her by as the years went on. Was this exactly what she wanted?

'I'll get back to the kitchen garden,' Mrs Barclay said tactfully, smiling at Helen. 'I've got some more hoeing to do, and there's a report of rain tonight, so I want to have it finished.'

'Is there anything I can do?' Helen demanded.

'No, dear. You've done quite enough today. Just sit there on the lawn and rest. I'm sure Russell can keep you occupied.'

'I'll do my poor best,' he replied with a grin. 'But your daughter doesn't need a lot of entertaining, Mrs Barclay. She's very easy to please.'

'That comes of being a nurse, I suppose,' Helen said, nodding, and again her mind thrust up a picture of Martin Reade. She wondered what was happining in her mind. Was there an evil influence at work inside her? And if so, where did it come from?

She sat down with Russell and they talked generally, but for most of the time Helen was having a tussle in her mind. She felt as if she had been bewitched by some gremlin that was out to torment her. She knew it had started when Russell kissed her, and she couldn't understand it. Studying him, all she could see was a tall, dark handsome man, very much to be desired by any normal girl. She remembered the pressure of his mouth against hers, and felt a tiny fluttering of desire start up inside. She breathed deeply and tried to control it with a fleeting thought of Martin, but that didn't seem to work, and she moistened her lips and leaned back to gaze at the evening sky through half closed eyes.

'I'd like to kiss you, Helen,' Russell said suddenly. 'Do you think your mother would mind if she saw us?'

'She's in the garden, and couldn't possibly see us,' Helen retorted immediately, before she was aware of what she was saying. The next instant Russell's mouth was against hers, compelling her to surrender, and she went limp against him, overpowered by his strange mastery. She was instantly filled with all the beautiful sensations that had invaded her the previous night out in the fields, and she put her arms around his neck and clung to him.

'Helen, I could lose my head over you,' he whispered into her attentive ear. 'I've never met a girl like you. I know the time is new yet, but I'm beginning to hope that you like Thorpe's Farm. You're exactly my type of girl, and I'm going to spend a lot of my free time with you.'

Helen did not know what to reply,

because she was weak and willing in his arms. She could not heed the warnings sounding in the back of her mind, for Russell was making her feel like a woman, lifting her up out of the rut of everyday life and its pressures and tensions. But vaguely she could hear an insistence that was making itself felt beyond the growing sensations. It seemed to speak with Martin's voice, and it told her that she ought to wonder about these kisses. She turned cold as she struggled inwardly to decide, and her aloofness communicated itself to Russell. He let her go with a laugh.

'I'm going too fast for you,' he said. 'I'll slow down, Helen, but I think the writing is on the wall as far as we're concerned.'

5

After Russell had departed later Helen went to bed with her mind troubled. While she had been with him she had been aware of the struggle that took place within her, as if good and bad were fighting for supremacy. But why did she feel like that? There was nothing sinister about Russell! He was a good companion, and very correct in his behaviour. Yet there had been something like a black shadow in the back of her consciousness, trying to warn her, filling her with doubt and taking away the pleasure she felt at being kissed by him. Was her subconscious mind picking up subtle impressions about him? Was there something in his background that sent out impulses to warn her of the consequences of becoming involved with him? She didn't know, and tried to ignore the alarms that raced through her.

She slept restlessly, and awoke in the morning with a slight headache and the feeling that she hadn't slept at all. When she looked out of the window she saw that rain was pelting down from a grey sky, and a strong breeze was driving the water hard at the flowers and tender green plants. She got dressed with a feeling of foreboding inside her, and went to see her mother, preparing breakfast. Mrs Barclay exclaimed at her strained expression.

'Are you feeling ill, Helen?' she demanded anxiously.

'No. I'm quite all right, Mother. But for some reason I didn't sleep well. I'll have a short nap after lunch, perhaps, and that should set me up again. What a dreadful day it is!'

She turned the conversation adroitly away from herself, and Mrs Barclay served breakfast. They talked of the coming day, of Helen's patients, and about Russell. Helen didn't want to talk about Russell, and the mention of his name started off a new train of thought in her mind. When she went out to the car with her case she was beginning to repeat the procedure of the day before, trying to analyze her mind, and with about as much failure as yesterday . . .

Before she could drive off Mrs Barclay appeared in the doorway, calling to her, and Helen guessed she was wanted on the telephone. She hurried back indoors and lifted the receiver. As she gave her name she told herself it would be Russell, and her heart seemed to lurch when she heard his voice in reply.

'I had to call you, Helen,' he said. 'What a rotten day for you! Are you about to leave?'

'I was in the car, Russell,' she replied. 'In another moment I would have been beyond recall.'

'Sorry. I'll make a note of the time and ring a little earlier in future. Don't get too wet, will you?'

'I'll try not to. But this is bad weather for farmers, isn't it?'

'No. We need rain sometimes, you

know. But I don't want to delay you, Helen. I really rang up to find out what you're doing this evening.'

'I don't think we'll have the chance to get together.' Helen didn't know why she lied. 'I think I'll be busy with that happy event I mentioned last night. You'll have to pass me up for tonight, Russell.'

'That's a great pity! I had great plans for tonight.' He sighed loudly. 'Never mind. As you said, it's one of the drawbacks of your profession. But it will keep for another night. What about tomorrow night?'

'I really can't say. It's all up to Nature, you know. This happy event may not take place for several days, and I'll have to stand by until it is all over.'

'All right. I'll let you get away now. See you sometime. Goodbye.'

'Goodbye, Russell!' Helen hung up with a feeling of relief inside her, and she wondered about it as she went out to the car. There was a great deal she just did not understand about herself. It was true that there were unplumbed depths in everyone, but she had always imagined herself to be open and above board. Her conduct surprised her. She had never felt or acted like this when she had known Harold.

She was thoughtful as she began her round, and the wet weather didn't bother her in the least. In fact it seemed to suit her mood, and she was thoughtful as she went from one patient to another. As the morning drew on she began to look hopefully for sign of Martin's car. She wanted to see him, to reassure herself about her feelings, to prove that she was not slipping under Russell's spell. But was she doing that? She could not explain the feelings that arose in her when she was with him, and a shiver passed through her as she recalled his kisses. When she was in his company she wanted to be kissed by him, but now, analyzing him, she felt a slight repugnance at having let herself go so wildly. It was badly out of character.

Helen was pleased, by lunch-time, to find that her day was going so smoothly despite the weather. There were no complications with any of her patients, and she wasn't held up anywhere. Going home to lunch, she learned that Martin had called, and for some unaccountable reason her pulses seemed to race when her mother mentioned his name.

'He's dropping by this evening, Helen,' Mrs Barclay said. 'He wants to see Mrs Pinner again. You'll be having her on your list tomorrow. She's got pneumonia, poor thing. She's seventy-two, and Doctor Reade says he daren't move her to hospital.'

'Oh dear! That sounds bad,' Helen said. 'Did he say what time he would be arriving?'

'At about seven. That should give you time to finish your round and have your tea.' Mrs Barclay sat down at the table, prepared to talk about the situation while they ate, and Helen felt she would rather listen than talk. But her mother was intent upon asking questions.

'Helen,' she began slowly. 'So much has happened since we arrived. We're settling down, and you're making froends. But tell me what you feel about Russell Thorpe.'

'You like him, don't you, Mother?' Helen countered.

'I do, but there's some strangeness about him I can't explain. It came to me on Sunday, although I didn't realize it at the time. When I was talking to Mrs Farrell about him while you and he were out walking, I had the feeling that she wasn't telling me the truth. You know I'm very sensitive about things like that. I told you the truth about Harold long before you discovered it.'

Helen frowned, only too aware of her own mixed feelings about Russell. But what could be wrong that would give off such intangible impressions? She shook her head slowly and considered her answer before replying.

'I find him very nice,' she said. 'Perhaps you're being a little too critical, Mother, after Harold.'

'Possibly, but I'd be careful where

he's concerned. He's too nice, Helen. He's too smooth and eager to please.'

'Perhaps you do him an injustice.' Helen continued with her meal. 'But what do you suspect?'

'I don't know!' Mrs Barclay shook her head. 'He's very friendly, and correct in his behaviour. But there is something at the back of it which will come to light before very long. How do you feel about Doctor Reade?'

Helen smiled thinly as she studied her mother's intent face. She could see concern in her features, and knew her mother was only worried about her welfare.

'I like Doctor Reade,' she replied. 'He's very nice! But you're not getting ideas about me already, are you? I'm sure Doctor Reade has his own circle of friends, and I doubt if I would fit into it very well.'

'That's why he wanted to take you out the other night,' Mrs Barclay said with a smile, and for some reason that she did not understand, Helen blushed.

'I'm taking too long over this meal,' Helen said quickly to change the subject. 'I've got quite a lot of ground to cover this afternoon, and I don't want to get home late. Save that apple pie for tea, Mother. I don't think I could face it now.'

Mrs Barclay nodded wisely, and Helen was relieved when she was ready to go about her business again. She found the rain had stopped when she started out, although the sky seemed filled with heavy, dragging clouds. Spring was blotted out for the present, and the strong breeze was shaking the blossoms off the trees and hedges.

The afternoon seemed to fly past, and Helen put it down to the fact that her thoughts were elsewhere. She did her work properly, and was cheerful to her patients, but inside she was struggling with impressions that would not subside. It was not like her to worry about anything, but since Sunday she was having difficulty to find peace of mind.

After tea she waited eagerly for Martin's arrival, and his car showed at the gate promptly at seven. She went to the door to answer his call, and he stepped inside for a moment.

'Hope I'm not disturbing you, Helen,' he said. 'How's Mrs Lovell?'

'I saw her this afternoon, and there's no change,' Helen reported. 'But I think I'll get the call any day now. Her happy event is due tomorrow.'

He nodded, his eyes not leaving her face. 'I'm going to see Mrs Pinner now,' he said. 'Did your mother tell you about her?'

'Yes. Is she seriously ill?'

'I daren't have her moved, and her age is against her. Would you like to come along with me to visit her?'

'Yes.' Helen nodded. 'I'll have to ring Mother every half hour, just in case Mrs Lovell decides to have her baby tonight. I'll just tell her where I'm going. Won't you go into the lounge?'

He smiled as he did so, and Helen carried with her a picture of his gentle brown eyes. She smiled softly to herself as she experienced a thrill. First Russell, now Martin! The thought stabbed through her. She was falling in love with the idea of romance. Perhaps she wanted to prove to herself that she was desirable. Harold's treatment of her must have harmed her sense of pride. But the deep, vibrant feelings that Russell aroused in her seemed to blanket her mind, preventing other, more normal impressions from taking root.

Mrs Barclay was pleased she was going out, and came to the door, greeting Martin cordially. Helen could see her mother was surveying Martin from a match-making point of view, and she hoped Martin couldn't interpret that dreamy expression on her mother's face.

Sitting with Martin in his car gave Helen a peacefulness she had not known since Sunday evening. She narrowed her eyes as she stared ahead. There was no way of breaking down and examining the pressures that had come to her from the moment Russell kissed her. But perhaps her own loneliness, which she had been successfully suppressing, was working against her and helping Russell. All she knew was that she needed all her strength of will to hold out against Russell's power.

But Martin exerted a gentle, persuasive manner upon her, and it did her good to sit beside him and feel reality coming slowly back to her mind. They began to chat about their work, and it was obvious that the common bond of their profession did much to make them feel at ease. Helen began to feel the soothing touch of his presence cooling down her thoughts, and by the time they reached their destination she was almost like her old self.

Mrs Pinner was showing some slight improvement, and after giving her an injection, Martin gave some encouragement to the daughter taking care of the old lady. When they departed, Helen rang her mother, and learned there were no calls for her. Martin began driving back to the bungalow, and Helen resumed her thoughts of the situation growing around her.

'Are you making friends locally?' Martin asked suddenly, and such was the note in his voice that Helen glanced at him with intent eyes.

'Yes,' she replied. 'Mother and I went to tea on Sunday to Thorpe's Farm. We had quite a nice time. Mother has become a member of the Women's Institute, and she and the housekeeper at the farm are going to work together on some of the Institute's projects. I'm so happy about that because life must be very dull for Mother, just keeping house for me and taking care of the calls.'

'And what about you, Helen?'

'Me?' She smiled. 'I'm too busy to make friends. I never was one for making friends, anyway.'

'What about boyfriends?' he persisted, and when she looked at him there was a smile upon his face. She could not help comparing him with Russell, and liking him all the more because of it.

'I've had one or two, but nothing serious,' she replied. 'I can see myself in thirty years' time, a dried up old spinster of a nurse, driving around these lanes and doing my duty as if there is nothing else in the world.'

'Is that what you want?'

'No, I don't think it is!' She spoke slowly, looking into his face. 'But I've got to the position where I think it's better to leave matters like that to the Gods. I think it's Fate, and it wouldn't do to interfere with the mysterious workings.'

'But it wouldn't hurt to help things along a little,' he argued. 'Take our situation, if you like. You're a young, unattached nurse and I'm a young, single doctor. In romantic novels we would have been in each other's arms in the first chapter, or I would at least have kissed you on our first meeting. But that will never come about if one of us doesn't push. The sort of thing that happens in books, like the heroine falling accidentally into the hero's arms, or he saves her from some impending disaster, doesn't really happen in real life, and one has to help the situation along if there's to be any progress.'

'I agree with you there,' she said with a smile. 'So what are you going to do? Are you going to throw aside your natural manner and act forward, like stopping the car on the verge and seizing me in your arms and kissing me until I suddenly realize that I'm madly in love with you?'

'I don't think I'd ever find the nerve to do that, or feel you'd accept it in the spirit in which it would be done. But unless I'm wrong, you're going to have to make it easier for me to see you when we're both off duty, Helen.'

'Yes.' She nodded slowly. 'I think I'd like that, Martin. You're off duty tomorrow evening, aren't you?'

'I am. May I call for you at about seven?'

'Yes, but with a reservation. There's Mrs Lovell, you know.'

'I know, and no doubt something will happen tomorrow evening. But if it does then we can attend the case together.'

'The doctor rarely puts in an appearance until after the baby is born,' Helen pointed out with a smile. 'Don't start a practice that may be frowned upon by your colleagues, Martin.'

'I won't. I don't think I'd let word of it get out. But I'll do anything to see you, Helen. It's lonely being a doctor with a country practice. I see you driving around sometimes, and I feel that we ought to get together. It's all very well being dedicated to our work, and we both are, you know, but we have to relax sometimes, and we both need to get away from it all.'

'You mentioned the village of Halesby,' Helen said. 'Shall we go there tomorrow evening, Mrs Lovell willing?'

'All right, it's a date.' He smiled and relaxed a little. 'What shall we talk about now?'

'Tell me something about yourself,' she demanded. 'I know very little of you.'

'There's not much to tell,' he replied with a thin laugh. 'I went through the usual years of studying. I spent three years in hospital routine, and now I'm a G.P., and enjoying it. I shall be quite happy staying in this area until I'm as old as Dr Arden. If I can I'll find a suitable girl and marry her.'

'Is there anyone on the short list for that appointment?' she demanded quickly.

'That would be telling,' he retorted.

Helen began to feel happy about him. He was a stranger, but then so was Russell, but he didn't have Russell's vibrant manner. He had a gentling effect upon Helen, and she liked it. Russell hit her like a storm at sea, and she didn't like that. It was disquieting to be mentally bombarded by some powerful magnetism that could not be defined. It was like being brain-washed, and she felt quite unsteady about it. If Russell hadn't begun to have that startling effect upon her she would have been more attracted to Martin, she realized. Perhaps it was a pity she had ever spoken to Russell.

It was obvious to her that while she was in Russell's company she couldn't fight against his advances. It was as if he stunned her natural mental defences. It was only when she was away from him that she could assert herself and try to place the whole matter into its proper perspective. But Martin was something of a resistance charger, and she welcomed his company, for being with him helped her recover from what seemed a sapping experience.

Before they reached the bungalow Martin slowed the car and ran off the road. Helen watched him as he switched off the engine. He smiled nervously, and glanced at his watch.

'We can steal five minutes from the day for ourselves,' he announced. 'I doubt I'll get a call in my absence, and in any case Dr Arden will be standing by, knowing I'm out on a case.'

Helen nodded, suddenly feeling tongue-tied. Her emotions had undergone a drastic change since she had arrived here. Most of it could be attributed to Russell's influence, but she was finding that Martin himself exerted certain pressures which were every bit as powerful. A silence developed against them, and the longer it lasted the more difficult, it seemed to Helen, to become. She turned from looking across the fields to find Martin watching her, and there was a faint smile on his lips.

'You haven't told me about yourself,' he said. 'I know where you came from, of course, and details of your training. I know your father is dead and that you live alone with your mother. But what about you, Helen? What makes you tick?'

'Perhaps I don't know the answer myself,' she retorted. 'I like my job, and until now I've lived for it. That sums me up in a nutshell. I'm finding life here very pleasant, and I like the country better than town. I expect there are grass roots somewhere in my background.'

'I'm the same,' he said. 'I love this part of the country. All through my training I longed for the time I could get back here.'

'And we arrived at about the same time,' she said.

'I find that very interesting,' he replied tensely. 'I think Fate has had a hand in it somewhere.'

'I think I'd like to think so,' Helen told him.

The silence enveloped them again, and she sighed. He watched her face closely, his own expressionless, although his eyes were bright. Slowly he reached out a hand and touched her shoulder. Helen caught her breath. She knew his intention, and would not stop him. Perhaps if he kissed her she would not feel Russell's personality so much.

'I think we'd better see if Fate has anything in store for us,' Martin said huskily. 'There's only one way to find out, Helen.'

'Yes,' she managed to say. Then her throat constricted and she was speechless. She went slowly into his arms, tilting her face to him, and his breath was warm on her cheek as he embraced her. She closed her eyes as their lips touched, and the first thing that became apparent was Martin's gentleness. There was none of the strong, he-man approach of Russell Thorpe here.

The silence was welcome now, and Helen found herself slipping down the long slope to ecstasy. Her desires quickened under his gentle touch, and she knew instantly that here was a man who could make her feel on top of the world. The power that Russell had exerted over her finally dissipated under new emotions stirring and strengthening inside her, and by the time they drew apart Helen knew she had learned something more about life. Her eyes were shining as she stared into his intent face.

'Well!' he declared. 'That was really something, Nurse Barclay. Perhaps it was most unprofessional of me, but doctors are only human, aren't they? Now what about the chances of Fate?'

'I think they stand a very good chance of proving something,' she said unsteadily. 'Thank you for showing me that, Martin.'

He laughed lightly, and the last ice between them was broken. Helen felt herself coming alive as she had never done before. Russell had awakened some deep impulses inside her that had nothing to do with love, and she could not begin to understand them, but Martin was totally different, and her mind seemed to be exclaiming about him in a way that far exceeded anything she ever felt for Harold. But Harold was dead and gone from her, his very existence exorcized by the religion of a new hope, and it wasn't Russell taking his place but Martin.

'I'd better not do that again or we'll never get back to your home,' he said. 'And what sort of gossip would spread about us, do you think, if someone saw us together in my car? We'd soon get bad reputations, wouldn't we?'

'I don't think I'd mind that,' she replied slowly.

'People would get hold of the wrong end of the stick,' he said, but his eyes showed that he was deeply affected by what had happened between them. 'I feel a little happier now,' he went on. 'I was beginning to think I didn't stand a chance of getting to know you, Helen.'

'Why?' She was intrigued by his words.

'It's hard to explain. There's something about you that says keep your distance.'

'Surely not!' She was thinking of Russell in that instant. He hadn't shown any similar feelings. He had taken hold of her and turned her world upside down. But she was getting his measure now, and she didn't want it to happen again. She realized with a start that she didn't want Russell to kiss her again, ever.

'It's just the impression I gained,' he

said. 'But I can see now that you are warm and alive, Helen.' He held her hand. 'I think we've both done the right thing by coming here to live and work.'

'And that's what I think,' she replied enthusiastically. 'I had the feeling before I arrived that everything would go right, and now I'm sure of it. Martin, I'm so glad you decided to come back to this district. Perhaps your faith in Fate is well placed.'

'I'm sure it is,' he retorted, his face alight with emotion. 'But its early days yet, and we have a lot of work on our hands to keep our minds well occupied. I only hope we'll find some free time occasionally, so that we can get together and come to know one another really well.'

'We can only try,' Helen replied, and sighed slowly. 'Now I suppose we'd better go. Time won't wait for us, and neither will Nature. There may be a call awaiting me, and I'd hate to get to Mrs Lovell too late.'

'That would never do,' Martin

agreed, and as he started the car something of their romantic mood died and allowed reality to come back and grasp them. But Helen would never forget the tenderness of their first kiss.

6

The next week seemed to speed by, and the Lovell baby arrived in the middle of the night, stealing most of Helen's sleep. But the confinement ended happily with a girl, which was exactly what Mrs Lovell wanted, and Helen drove homewards later with the joy of knowing that she had brought another life into the world. It was the third birth since her arrival, and she thought deeply as she drove through the growing greyness of approaching day. In thirty years that small figure of three would swell to hundreds, no doubt even higher, and she stifled a yawn as she parked the car and let herself quietly into the bungalow and went wearily to her bed. She might be able to get three hours sleep! Then she would be up and away attending her patients.

She didn't see anything of Russell,

although he telephoned each morning. Until the Lovell baby arrived Helen used that as an excuse for not going out with Russell, but afterwards she could not keep him at bay for long. She went out with Martin on the night after he had kissed her, and they visited the local beauty spot at the village of Halesby. They had a wonderful evening, and Helen was sorry when it ended. But she had to face reality, and in this case it was Russell Thorpe. On the Saturday morning he called as usual, and Helen had to answer.

'Helen, I haven't seen you for most of this week,' he complained. 'What's happening? You're not as busy as all that, are you? I heard that the Lovell baby arrived. Are you trying to avoid me?'

'Of course not!' she replied, and wished she had the courage to tell him the truth. 'But a nurse's life in the country is a very hectic one, and I had to make up for lost time because of visiting you last Sunday.' She hoped the lie would put him off, but he was made of sterner stuff.

'I can't believe that! You are trying to avoid me! I'll have to come and see you this evening.'

'Please, Russell, you'll be making the trip for nothing. I have two evening calls to make tonight. One patient is extremely ill and likely to die. I shall have to sit with her, I'm afraid.'

'Why hasn't the doctor taken her into hospital?' he demanded. 'That isn't part of your work, Helen, surely!'

'I have to do as I'm told,' she replied.

'All right, I'll believe you this once. But I'll want to see you sometime tomorrow, you know.'

'I had an easy day last Sunday,' she said, 'but that cannot always be relied upon.'

'So you don't have any social life at all.' He tut-tutted. 'I don't like the sound of that. Would you ever give up that work, Helen?'

'No!' She spoke quickly and decisively. 'This is my whole life, Russell.'

'Then I shall have to get used to it,' he asserted. 'I'll see you later, Helen.'

Before she could object he had rung off, and she replaced the receiver and stood for a moment staring down at the infernal instrument that controlled her life. Could she put Russell off without hurting his feelings? Would he slowly drift away from her if she happened to be busy each time he wanted to see her or take her out? She didn't think so. He was so persistent, and seemed to know all the answers. When she thought of the way she had allowed him to kiss her she almost blushed in shame. Whatever had come over her, it had been only a temporary lapse. Since she had stayed out of his sight and reach her feelings had returned to normal, but she was afraid the weakness would return if he came back into her life. But if he did she would have to ensure that they were never alone.

She pondered over his strange power as she started her round that Saturday morning. Everything went well. She could do her work with only a part of her mind concentrating upon it, and she didn't waste any time. Her only cause for alarm was the patient she had told Russell she might have to sit with. It was an old man, well into his eighties, who had fallen from a chair, and Martin feared pneumonia was setting in. The patient's son, with whom he lived, had refused to let the old man go into hospital, and there was little anyone could do about it. If the old man was going to die then he would do so in his little cottage where he had lived out most of his life.

The old man seemed about the same when Helen looked in upon him, and she learned that Martin hadn't called yet. She kept watching for Martin as she went on with her round, but sometimes their routes were wide apart, and this morning they were not destined to meet. But when she parked in the village of Suffling she had hardly alighted from the car when Russell pulled in behind her. She felt her heart sink as she stared at him, but a slow smile started across her lips.

'Hello, Russell, she greeted as he got out of the car. 'Are you following me?'

'I have been looking around in the hope of seeing you,' he admitted. 'Are you terribly busy? I wanted to show you some new calves. They were born last night. If you've never seen a calf at their age you don't know what you've been missing. Remember the foals last Sunday?'

'Do I!' Helen nodded, filled with pleasure at the memory. 'But I am so busy today, Russell. I just can't spare the time.'

'I thought as much, so what about tomorrow?'

'I shall be on call, but if I do find the time perhaps I'll drop by. Will that be all right?'

'If that's the best you can do then I'll have to be satisfied with it,' he replied. He came closer, and Helen found that she cringed from him. 'I wish I could kiss you,' he said. 'It seems ages since I last did that.'

'Russell, I don't usually behave like that,' she said firmly. 'Perhaps it was the magic of the scenery, or something, that sent me into your arms last Sunday, but I feel uncomfortable about it, and I don't want you to kiss me again.'

'What's in a kiss?' he demanded. 'You enjoyed it, didn't you?' He smiled, his dark eyes seeming to glow. Before she could answer he went on quickly. 'Don't tell me you didn't enjoy it because I know you did. So what's all the fuss about? You need some enjoyment in your life, you know. All work and no play makes Jack a dull boy! I suppose the same applies to Jill. What's wrong Helen? Have I offended you in some way? I'm really sorry if there is something. But after last Sunday I thought you had taken a liking to me!'

'Russell, it isn't anything like that,' she said quickly. 'Please don't think it is! We're hardly more than strangers, you know, despite last Sunday, and some girls are a little shy.'

'Is that it?' He nodded as he studied

her face, and she could feel the tug of his personality. She felt as if her feet were set upon a slippery path, and one wrong step would upset her completely. What was there about him that did this to her? And did he know about this strange power which he possessed? He smiled thinly. 'I'll give you more time,' he said reluctantly. 'But I thought we were doing very well together, Helen.'

'I'm sorry, but I'll have to go, Russell,' she said. 'I daren't get behind with the round.'

'All right,' he said grudgingly, and although he smiled there was little humour in him. 'Don't work too hard, will you?'

'I do my best to keep up with it,' she replied, and tightened her grip upon her case and went on her way. She was aware that his bold dark eyes followed her every movement, and she felt uncomfortable as she entered a garden and hurried to the door of a house. She wanted to get out of his gaze.

The woman who let her into the

house studied her face closely, and Helen saw her looking out through the doorway at Russell as he drove away. The woman shut the door with a bang, and studied Helen's face before leading the way up the stairs to where her husband lay in bed with a badly injured leg, which he had stuck with a pitch-fork.

'Are you friendly with the likes of Russell Thorpe, Nurse?'

'I know him, Mrs Cargill,' Helen replied. 'Why do you ask?'

'Seeing that you're a stranger around here and might not know about him.' Mrs Cargill broke off and closed her mouth firmly. 'Perhaps I'm talking out of turn.'

'Not at all.' Helen was intrigued. 'Please go on with what you were saying.'

'I reckon not. My husband tells me I've always got too much to say for myself. But you be ruled by me and don't get too friendly with Farmer Thorpe.'

'I don't understand you,' Helen said as they ascended the stairs.

But they were on the point of entering the bedroom, and the woman wouldn't say anything in front of her husband. Helen dressed the man's wound, and listened to his chatter, answering his interested questions smoothly and without hesitation, but her mind was busy turning over what the woman had said, and when they left the bedroom and Helen was being shown out she could not resist attempting to get Mrs Cargill to enlarge upon what she had said.

'I'm not a troublemaker, Nurse,' the woman said, shaking her head. 'I'm not going to say anything. Words such as I could say have a habit of coming back upon the speaker's head. I don't want any of that.'

'I see.' Helen didn't know what to make of it. 'I go around helping a lot of people,' she said. 'If you know something that might help me then I'm sure you ought to talk about it.'

'Mostly gossip, Nurse, and likely

there isn't a grain of truth in any of it.'

'Perhaps you'll tell me and let me be the judge of it.' For some reason Helen wanted to know what was on the woman's mind. 'I don't pay any heed to gossip, Mrs Cargill, but a friendly word of warning never hurt anyone.'

'There are plenty around as would tell you all about it,' came the slow reply. 'But I've said too much already. Good day, Nurse. Will you be calling tomorrow?'

'Yes, Mrs Cargill.' Helen turned away, and a frown came to her face as she went back to her car. Was there some breath of scandal about Russell? If so why hadn't she heard of it before? And what could it possibly be? She was thoughtful as she went on. She was recalling her own feelings about him, and remembering what her mother had said. If anyone was a good judge of character it was her mother, and Helen tried to settle her suspicions as she continued with her round.

By lunch time she was seething with

curiosity, and wanted to get to the bottom of the mystery. That much she knew instinctively. She couldn't go against her instincts, and they had warned her at the very beginning. Something was not quite right.

Mrs Barclay had a message for her when she arrived home. Martin had telephoned to say that he would be calling during the evening, and Helen felt a flush of pleasure, a pang of pure joy that could not be harmed by the darker thoughts of Russell Thorpe that lurked within.

'What sort of a morning has it been, dear?' Mrs Barclay asked anxiously as they sat down to lunch.

'I haven't stopped for a moment,' Helen replied, 'but that's the way to be, isn't it?'

'You can do too much,' her mother warned. 'But you do have a good person in Doctor Reade to help you relax. I'm glad to see that you're dropping Russell, Helen.'

'Why, Mother? 'Helen met her

mother's steady gaze across the table.

'I don't know exactly, but you recall that we both said we didn't like his background manner.'

'That isn't it exactly, and you know it,' Helen said. 'Have you been hearing stories about Russell, Mother?'

'Stories?' Mrs Barclay exclaimed.

'Yes, and don't deny it,' Helen pursued. 'I know you well enough to tell when you're trying to warn me about something while keeping the details away. What is it?'

'What sort of stories could be going around about Russell?' Mrs Barclay demanded.

'Suppose you tell me?' Helen offered.

'Well Mrs Miller, the butcher's wife, called with the meat this morning. She does all her husband's deliveries with a van, you know. She heard that we went to the farm last week end for tea, and she wanted to warn us against Russell.'

'But you don't believe the warning was genuine,' Helen said.

'Why not?' her mother demanded.

'Because you didn't pass it on to me,' Helen said patiently. 'I almost received a warning myself from a Mrs Cargill. She saw Russell talking to me outside her house. Now what is this story that I haven't heard yet?'

'It's to do with a girl,' Mrs Barclay said stiffly. 'That was why I wanted to keep it away from you for as long as possible.'

'I don't see why. I'm not a child to be protected from sordid stories.'

'I know that, dear, but the details might have upset you, seeing that you like Russell.'

'Get to the point, Mother,' Helen commanded. 'You know I don't have much time.'

'The girl committed suicide, Helen, because Russell wouldn't marry her. He had promised, so the story goes, but when the time came he jilted her, and she drowned herself in the river.'

'That's dreadful,' Helen said stiffly, 'but I don't see why a warning need be issued.' She sighed as she considered what her mother had said. 'I don't suppose Russell was to blame for the girl's end. No doubt he didn't think she would do away with herself.'

'You're defending him! Does that mean you have some feelings for him?' Mrs Barclay watched Helen anxiously.

'Not at all! But I don't like gossip. These local legends are based on truth, I admit, but much of their substance is fictitious. What else is being said?'

'There is more to it. There are rumours that the girl didn't jump into the river.'

'What do you mean?'

'They say she was pushed.' Mrs Barclay was deadly serious.

'Really, Mother! You ought to know better than to listen to such talk. Even if there was the slightest truth in it I don't see why I have to be warned against him. He doesn't mean anything to me. He's not going to get me into such a state that suicide is the only way out.'

'One can't be too careful, Helen. You're out at all hours of the day and night. If he's as deep as they say then there's no telling what his passions will lead him into.'

'That's quite enough of that,' Helen said firmly. 'You'll have me afraid to go out in the dark if you keep this up, Mother, and I shan't like leaving you alone in the house.'

'I don't think he'd bother with me.' Mrs Barclay shook her head. 'But I did tell you there was something about him that I didn't like, didn't I?'

Helen did not reply, and ate her lunch, but her thoughts were moving fast. She could not forget the way Russell had commanded her emotions. It was as though he had — she paused to consider the word that came to her mind — hypnotized her! She breathed heavily, wondering about him in the light of the story her mother had told her. Was there any truth in it? Her own words about rumours containing a smattering of truth came back to roost, and she shook her head and sighed. She wouldn't listen to hearsay, and in any case it didn't matter to her because she was not interested in him. She knew beyond all doubt that if there was a man alive who could become important to her then it was Martin.

'What was the verdict of the girl's inquest?' she asked suddenly as she finished her meal. 'Did you hear that, Mother?'

'Yes.' Mrs Barclay nodded. 'No blame was attached to Russell. The verdict was suicide whilst the balance of the mind was disturbed. But she was also in trouble, Helen.'

'That doesn't point to Russell's guilt, Mother!' Helen spoke sharply. 'He suddenly refused to marry her, the story has it, didn't he?'

'That's right.'

'Then it might prove his innocence rather than his guilt, 'Helen said.

'That's possible.' Mrs Barclay was clearly disturbed. 'I don't know why Mrs Farrell didn't say anything to me about it.'

'Loyalty, I expect.' Helen smiled. 'If

she is loyal to him then you can take it there must be some good in him.'

'I don't care what you say, I'm happy that you're not interested in him, dear,' Mrs Barclay said for a parting shot. 'When shall I see you again, Helen?'

'Some time during the late afternoon, I expect,' Helen replied. 'Don't listen to too many stories while I'm away, Mother. You'll spoil my tea!'

'Sorry, dear, but it was something I thought you ought to know about.'

'Perhaps you're right. We'll think about it and discuss it later, if you like. But really it's got nothing to do with us and does not touch upon our knowing Russell.'

Helen left to resume her round, but she found her mind heavy with speculation. No doubt Mrs Cargill had been alluding to the same story when she almost talked to her that morning. It wasn't a pleasant story! But Helen couldn't really believe that Russell was as bad as they had painted him. One could usually tell. But no one could say what happened between him and the girl who died. The talk that perhaps Russell had pushed her into the river — murdered her — was just so much gossip spread by sensationalists. The police would have gone through the case very thoroughly, she had no doubt. But despite her self-assurances, Helen still felt decidedly suspicious about Russell, and put it down to the way his strange power had affected her. She could well understand any girl becoming emotionally involved with such a man.

She felt uneasy as she returned home later, and although she put a cheerful expression upon her face she could not prevent her tiredness showing through. But a hot cup of tea picked her up a little and she began to look forward to seeing Martin. She had a call to make, as she had explained earlier to Russell, but it would not keep her as long as she made out. No doubt Martin would go with her, and afterwards they could spend a few quiet minutes together.

That thought appealed to her. She felt a thrill speed through her as she recalled the way he had kissed her before. Despite Russell's great power he could not move her in exactly the way that Martin did. She realized that having Martin now helped her resist Russell. Until Martin showed interest in her she had been completely under Russell's spell.

She was tired, but a shower did much to revive her, and when Martin arrived she was dressed in a flowery summer dress and feeling quite comfortable.

'You look very fetching in your uniform,' Martin said softly as she opened the door to him, 'but seeing you like this makes all the difference. It's quite surprising how different you look in casual dress. You're not so formidable.'

'Do I strike you as formidable?' she demanded with a smile.

'Not exactly that,' he mused. 'It's more your cool efficiency. It makes a mere man feel out of place holding romantic thoughts about you.'

'Really? I'm sorry to hear that! It seems as if I'm going to lose something through being good at my job. That's hardly fair, is it?'

'I'll do something about it, Helen,' he urged. 'I'm only fooling! But you do look good enough to eat.'

She smiled. 'You know I have a call to make this evening, don't you?'

'Yes. That's partly why I'm here. I want to go with you, and afterwards we can forget that you're a nurse and I'm a doctor and go off somewhere to enjoy ourselves.'

'Like we did at Halesby,' she said eagerly, and her blue eyes sparkled. 'I'm never going to forget that evening, Martin.'

'Good. I'm glad you enjoyed yourself because I have plans for more times just like that one.'

'I'll have to telephone Mother later,' she said.

'I know! I think we ought to get you a radio-telephone for your car, you know.

That would save a lot of trouble.'

Helen went to find her mother and to tell her that she was about to leave.

'Is Martin here?' Mrs Barclay demanded.

'Yes, he's just arrived. We have a call to make, and afterwards we're going for a drive, but I'll call you later.'

'Have a nice time, dear!' Mrs Barclay smiled knowingly. 'I think you're doing the right thing, Helen.'

'What's that, Mother?' she demanded innocently.

'Making a good friend of Doctor Reade. You know perfectly well what I mean!'

Helen smiled as she took her leave, and she picked up her case from the hall and went for Martin. He took the case from her and they went out to his car. As they reached it a large car pulled in behind, and Helen turned to see Russell Thorpe getting out of it. Her heart seemed to miss a beat as she took in his tense expression, and she breathed deeply as she glanced at Martin.

'Not more business!' Martin exclaimed.

'I don't think so,' Helen said in wavering tones. 'This is Russell Thorpe, Martin. You know, Thorpe's Farm. Russell, this is Doctor Martin Reade.'

'How do you do?' Russell said coolly, looking them over in a way that made Helen want to curl up. 'I had heard Doctor Arden took on some help.'

'How do you do?' Martin replied.

'We're just going out on a call,' Helen said quickly, and she saw a glint come into Russell's eyes.

'In that dress?' Russell demanded. 'Don't you wear uniform after tea?'

'Not if I can help it,' Helen said. 'You will excuse us, Russell, we are in a hurry.'

'Very well!' He shook his head as if arguing with himself over something beyond their knowledge. 'You did tell me you would be busy this evening, didn't you?'

'I did.' Helen sighed as she turned away. She had kept her voice expressionless, but she did not miss the look that Martin gave her, or the tension that came into Russell's eyes. For one awful moment she thought Russell was going to say something about their past meetings, and the expression which came to his weathered face was positively ugly. But he smiled and stepped aside, and Martin helped Helen into his car and then unhurriedly went around to his side. Helen did not look back at Russell as they drove off, but she had a good idea of the sort of thing passing through his mind, and the stories she had heard about him flared in her mind, making her imagine that all of them were true. She shuddered as they went on down the lane, and didn't know why she should feel so affected . . .

7

Helen felt awkward for some time as Martin drove on, and he was silent. She dared not even look at him for fear of catching his eye. Her throat was constricted and she knew she would sound terrible if she tried to speak. Swallowing didn't seem to help her, and she cast around in her mind for something to say that would make everything sound normal. But it was Martin who broke the silence, and his tones were even and controlled, giving no hint of what he was thinking.

'Doctor Arden was saying this evening how well you seem to have settled down in this job, Helen.'

'Really?' She risked a glance at him, and found that he was staring straight ahead. 'Well I always do my best, Martin.'

'And that best is considerable,' he

retorted. 'All the patients he's spoken to have nothing but praise for the way you handle them, and there was a lot of talk before you started, so Doctor Arden informs me, about no one being able to take the place of Nurse Griffin.'

'I did hear some of that myself, but it seems to have died away in the last two weeks.' Helen smiled, feeling herself returning to normal. Talking shop was the best thing they could do, she realized, and wondered frantically if she ought to mention Russell Thorpe now. She decided against it. Martin himself would broach the subject if he wanted to know anything, and just before they made their call on the patient he did touch fleetingly on the matter.

'You did say you went to Thorpe's Farm for tea, didn't you?' he asked.

'Yes. It was last Sunday.'

'I've heard that the local people are complaining about him.'

'Really! What about?' Helen tensed despite herself.

'That pond in his meadow by the

main road. The villagers say they can't keep their children away from it.'

'I mentioned that to him myself,' Helen said, breathing a bit easier. 'I made some suggestions, but he evidently hasn't paid any heed to them.'

'He's not a responsible type of person, from all accounts,' Martin said, and left it at that.

They arrived at the patient's house soon after, and Helen was glad of the diversion. They attended to the patient, and shortly afterwards went on their way. But Helen had the feeling that the evening had been spoiled by Russell's appearance at her home. For her at any rate there was an atmosphere of tension, although Martin kept up a light chatter. But she sensed that he was thinking about Russell, and she herself was tempted time and again from Martin's company to think of the man. That strange power still retained its potency, despite Martin's presence.

At the end of the evening Helen felt that it had all been a failure. Martin made no attempt to kiss her, and on their homeward drive she began to look forward to the moment when he would park the car and take her into his strong arms. But he didn't. He drove to her gate and stopped, switching off the engine before turning to look at her.

'I expect you must be tired after your day's work,' he said. 'I know I feel it at the end of the day.' His tones were normal, and Helen found it difficult to believe that he was in some kind of a mood because of Russell Thorpe. Was it just her imagination? She couldn't say, and she reached for her case and opened her door.

'I am tired,' she said softly. 'But thank you for taking me out. I have enjoyed myself.'

'Good. I'm glad.' He didn't sound too happy, but he smiled. 'I'll see you tomorrow perhaps. I expect we'll meet on our rounds.'

'I hope so.' She smiled as she alighted, and she closed the door and stepped back. For a moment he held her eyes, then he lifted a hand as he pulled away. Helen waved to him, smiling bravely, and then he was gone, and she sighed heavily as she turned in at the gate. Russell had spoiled the evening! It wasn't what he had said, but the fact that he had shown himself. That was how powerful his personality seemed to be. But had it affected Martin as well? Or had Martin thought she had been encouraging Russell?

Helen was glad her mother had gone to bed. She went into the bungalow and put down her case, deciding against having supper. She prepared to go to bed, and there was a sinking feeling inside her as she lay down in the dark and closed her eyes. But sleep wouldn't come at her bidding, and she slowly lost her tiredness and opened her eyes. She stared around the room, trying to induce sleep, and the harder she tried the worse it became. Eventually she sighed and sat up. It was Russell again, his personality firing her imagination. Those stories about him! They had to be true. She herself knew how forceful he was. He must have twisted that poor girl's mind into a terrible state for her to commit suicide! But rumour had it that she had been pushed into the river! An ominous pang stabbed through Helen, and lying in the darkness with her thoughts keeping her awake, she could not fight her forming opinions. Russell seemed to be the type who would act drastically in any situation.

When she did sleep it was badly, and she awoke in the morning feeling haggard and weary. Her mind was filled with conjecture, and she seemed nervy. As she was eating breakfast the telephone rang, and she started nervously, sighing as her mother went in answer. Then she realized why she was feeling pent up. Russell usually rang in the mornings, and this morning she felt loath to speak to him. She waited tensely for her mother's return, and drank her tea slowly, her mind far from what she was doing.

'It was Doctor Arden's receptionist,'

Mrs Barclay announced, coming back into the kitchen. 'I've made a note of the new patients to go on your list, Helen, and it's lying beside the telephone. Don't forget it when you go, will you?'

'I'll make a new list myself, and include them in it,' Helen said.

'Did you enjoy yourself last evening?' her mother wanted to know.

'Yes, very much. Martin is such good company.'

'I saw Russell arrive as you went out. What did he want?'

'Just passing.' Helen smiled, glad that she was able to fake a light tone.

'There's a great deal of difference between those two men,' her mother went on, and Helen glanced at her watch, relieved that it was almost time to depart. I'm glad you haven't taken a great liking to Russell, although last week I thought you were going to.'

'I don't think he's my type,' Helen said with a smile. 'He seems too intense.'

'It's strange he's never married, and he doesn't seem to have any interest in girls,' her mother mused. 'However Doctor Reade seems to have taken you in hand. I've got no complaints about him, Helen, and I hope you'll like him.'

'I do,' Helen admitted. 'He's very nice.' She glanced at her watch again. 'I must run now, Mother. See you at lunch.'

'Mind how you go,' Mrs Barclay said.

As she went into the hall the telephone rang, and Helen's heart seemed to sink. She stood listening to it for a moment, and her mother came quickly, looking puzzled.

'Aren't you going to answer it, dear?' she demanded.

'You answer it,' Helen said slowly, and touched her mother's arm in passing. 'If it's Russell would you tell him I've just left?'

'Yes, dear, if you want me to.' The puzzlement still showed on Mrs Barclay's face as she went to the instrument, and Helen stood waiting tensely, watching her mother's features with narrowed eyes. 'Yes, Russell,' Mrs Barclay said slowly in answer to the voice at the other end of the wire. 'I'm sorry but you're just too late. I heard Helen's car going along the lane as you rang. Is there a message I can give her?'

Helen waited, hearing the rasp of Russell's voice but being unable to make out what he said. Her mother listened for some time, nodding occasionally, her eyes lifting to Helen's face, and when their glances met Mrs Barclay pulled a face at her daughter. Finally she hung up, and Helen waited for a report on what was said.

'He wants you to call and see Mrs Farrell, if you would,' Mrs Barclay said. 'It seems that she's had a fall this morning, and won't let him call for the doctor. She's at a bad age to be tumbling about. Can you fit her in, Helen?'

'If she's as bad as that the doctor ought to be called,' Helen said. 'But I'll see what I can do.'

'She might have broken a bone. You'd better not delay. I don't like the sound of it, Helen.'

'I'll work my way towards the farm,' Helen said. 'I'll tell him that I rang you after being out a while and you told me about it.'

'Don't make it too long, just in case,' Mrs Barclay said.

Helen nodded and took her leave, feeling happier because she hadn't spoken to Russell. It was strange how he had affected her, made her feel that she was beginning to fall in love with him. But then Martin had come into the picture, and from that moment she had begun to regard Russell with an emotion akin to distaste, and it wasn't because of the stories she'd heard. Of that she was more than certain.

She drove quickly into the village, and made a round of the patients there before considering going on. Then she drove to Thorpe's Farm, and wondered where Russell was as she drew up before the large house. For some obscure reason she didn't want to face him, but he appeared in the doorway as she walked towards it, and there was a flickering smile of welcome upon his face as she reached him.

'So glad you could make it,' he said, opening the door wide. 'I suppose you rang your home from the village, did you?'

'I always do before going on to the next, just in case there is a late call. It saves having to come all the way back later.'

'A good idea. But do come in. Poor Mrs Farrell is sore from her fall. I don't think any serious damage has been done, but it always best to have an opinion at her age.'

'Where is she?' Helen entered the house.

'I put her in one of the downstairs rooms,' he replied. 'She wouldn't go back to bed, and wanted to get on with her work. But I insisted that she rests until you've seen her. She wouldn't let me send for the doctor.'

'Old people can be very stubborn,' Helen said conversationally as they walked along the wide hall. She held her breath as he glanced at her, and could feel the insistent drumming of his personality at work on her.

'Mrs Farrell is one of the best,' he retorted. 'I wouldn't want anything to happen to her.'

The old housekeeper was stretched out on a long couch, and she looked pale and shocked when Helen saw her, although a thin smile touched her lips.

'Hello, Mrs Farrell. What have you been up to?' Helen demanded cheerfully.

'It's nothing to worry about,' came the disgruntled reply. 'I told him I didn't want any fuss made.'

'But you can't go falling about like a two-year-old,' Helen said, crossing to the woman's side. 'Do you hurt anywhere?'

'Nowhere in particular. I haven't broken anything, so I don't know what all the fuss is about.'

'You're a very important person in this household,' Helen said warmly. 'It's only right that Russell takes good care of you.' She glanced around to see that he hadn't followed her into the room, and the door was closed. That relieved her somewhat, and she sat down on the couch at Mrs Farrell's side. 'I do think you ought to have the doctor to see you, Mrs Farrell, 'she commented. 'You're shocked by the fall. That much is evident. I don't think you ought to get on your feet again at all today. I'll get Russell to help me carry you to your room.'

'I'm not going to bed, so don't try to make me. There's too much to be done around here.'

Helen could see she would get no co-operation from the woman, and she shook her head. Mrs Farrell tried to get up off the couch, but when she put her right foot to the floor she groaned and fell back, gasping for breath.

'So you have hurt yourself,' Helen said. 'Now you just do as I tell you, Mrs

Farrell. Where does it hurt?'

'My ankle,' the old lady said through her teeth. 'I think I've twisted it.'

Helen examined the ankle in question, and shook her head, looking into the housekeeper's eyes. 'I'm afraid you've done more than that. It's fractured, Mrs Farrell.'

'Does that mean I'll have to go to the hospital?' the woman wailed.

'I'm afraid so. We can't take any chances with you. I expect they'll keep you in for a day or two until you recover from the shock. Now you're not to worry. They'll take very good care of you.'

'I don't want to leave him alone in the house,' Mrs Farrell said. 'Who's going to look after him while I'm away?'

'I'm sure Russell is capable of taking care of himself!' Helen covered the old lady with the blanket that Russell had put around her. 'Now you keep off that foot, won't you? I'll go and phone the doctor. He'll be coming into the district very soon. I expect you will have to go into hospital, so don't think that you can stay here.'

She went out of the room, and found Russell waiting in the hall. He turned to her with a look of enquiry upon his face, and Helen shook her head slightly.

'I think she's got a fractured ankle,' she said. 'She's suffering from shock. I expect she'll be taken into hospital. May I use your phone?'

'Certainly.' He nodded. 'There it is.' He motioned towards a tall table by the foot of the stairs. 'This is a bad business. Her age is against her.'

'That's why you ought to have rung for the doctor as soon as it happened,' Helen said severely.

'I like you when you're busy at your work,' he said, following her to the telephone, and he stood very close to her while she made the call to the doctor's surgery. The receptionist promised to let Martin know about the case as soon as possible, and Helen was relieved when she hung up.

'Will you take care of Mrs Farrell

until Doctor Reade arrives?' she asked.

'Of course. That's why I'm here now. I ought to have been at market today, but I've sent my manager instead. Don't you worry about Mrs Farrell. She's like a mother to me, and I'll take very good care of her.'

'I have to get on with my round,' Helen said. 'If I wasn't so busy I'd wait until the doctor arrives, but I must go. However I'll have a word with her. She'll need some reassuring before she goes to hospital.'

'I'd like to talk to you before you go, Helen,' he said, and took her arm as she turned back to the room. 'I want to talk to you about us.'

'Us?' she repeated. 'I don't understand, Russell.'

'That's why I want to talk,' he retorted. There was a smile on his face, but there was nothing pleasant about it.

Helen drew a sharp breath as she went into the room, and he followed her. She could feel a weakening inside her, and knew his strange power was at work. Was it in his eyes? They seemed to hold a hypnotic stare. Was he deliberately trying to influence her? She forced herself to concentrate upon her work, and that seemed to help. But she wouldn't be happy until she was back on her round again. It was in her mind that there was something evil in the aura that surrounded him, and it made her feel uneasy as she tried to comfort Mrs Farrell and prepare the woman for going to hospital. Russell remained silent in the background, and Helen was intensely aware of his presence.

'You don't have to fuss around me, Helen,' Mrs Farrell said gravely. 'Get you on and look after your other patients. 'I'll be all right. Russell will take care of me.'

Helen nodded, and after satisfying herself that the housekeeper would be all right until Martin arrived she took her leave. Russell followed her out to the car.

'Helen, what's wrong?' he demanded.

'Wrong?' she repeated, shaking her

head. 'What do you mean?'

'There's a change in you since last Sunday.'

'I thought I explained that,' she said. 'You promised not to be so bold.'

'That was all right as far as it went,' he continued. 'But there is this doctor coming into the picture. Are you sure he isn't cutting me out?'

'Russell, that isn't a proper thing to say! Doctor Reade is my boss to all intents and purposes, and last night when you saw us we were on our way to a case.'

'And afterwards?' he persisted.

'I must go,' she said quickly. I'm behind with my work as it is.'

'I feel there's something going on,' he said. 'I don't like it, Helen.'

'Russell, perhaps you're taking too much for granted,' she replied with determination in her voice.

'I don't think so.' He smiled, and the sunlight found a glitter in his eyes. 'When may I see you again?'

'I shall be busy for several days,' she

said cautiously, hoping that the passage of time would put him off.

'But you can't be working all the time. Surely you get evenings off.'

'If I don't have to visit patients again in the same day then I do find some time for myself. But usually I have a lot to do at home, to do with nursing. There are forms to be filled in and all manner of tasks that consume time.'

'In other words there's no room for me in your life, is that it?'

She raised her eyes to his face, wanting dearly to agree with him, but somehow the words would not form on her lips. She shook her head slowly. 'It isn't that at all, Russell, and you know it. Please try to understand.'

'I think I do understand.' He nodded slowly. 'Don't let me keep you from your work, Helen. I'd better get back to Mrs Farrell. Thank you for calling.'

Helen stared at him, wondering at the change in his manner, and she could feel his power working at full blast. She didn't want to hurt him! She didn't want him to misunderstand! Those thoughts were uppermost in her mind, and she realized that he was causing her to have them. She took a deep breath as she turned away from him, and it required a mental effort to do so. She got into her car, conscious of the fact that he was staring at her. She felt a strange prickling sensation along her spine, and shuddered as she started the engine. It was more than time to go, and the sooner she got away from here the better. But she lifted a hand in farewell and waved to him, seeing him reply as she drove off. She was silent as she resumed her round. Her mind seemed strangely weary of thoughts.

The rest of the morning passed pleasantly, and she made up the time she had lost. Some of the houses where she called were little more than country cottages, and some of the occupants had lived in the same place for most of their lives. They were a patient, pleasant people in the main, always ready to talk about the past and the village, and

Helen enjoyed the moments she stole to stay on and listen.

After lunch she went on to the outer villages of her district, and the afternoon passed pleasantly enough. In Suffling she saw Martin's car, and pulled in beside it. He was visiting a house next to one where she was calling, and she waited until he emerged. He smiled cheerily when he saw her, and she hoped the mood of the previous evening had gone for good.

'Hello,' he greeted gently. 'It seems that I've been following you all day. I went to see Mrs Farrell just before lunch, and she's gone into hospital. She's suffering badly from shock, although she maintains that she's perfectly all right. Some of these people are really tough, Helen.'

'That's what I've discovered,' she replied. 'But they're all very nice. I don't think I'd change this district for anything, Martin.'

'There's one exception,' he added slowly.

'Russell Thorpe?' she demanded,

reading his face.

'Yes.' He sighed heavily. 'He warned me to stay away from you, Helen.'

'Oh no!' Her expression changed. 'Martin, what must you think of this?'

'But nothing at all,' he retorted. 'He struck me as being a very forward man, and I'm surprised you haven't had trouble from him. I don't know what your feelings are towards him, and if you do have any hopes in that direction then I'll stay strictly away from you. But he has no right to talk like that if you've not given him any encouragement.'

'Encouragement! Martin, I've been trying to keep him off my neck!'

'Is that a fact?' He smiled then, and his expression cleared. 'Well in that case I'll know how to treat him if he talks to me again. I must admit that I was a little puzzled last night when he turned up at your home. He was so familiar! I just didn't know where I stood'

'Well you can take it from me that I don't like him, Martin. I sense something deep about him that makes me wonder. I don't think I'd like to be alone in his company after dark.'

'There is talk about him around the villages, did you know?'

'About a girl?' she demanded, and he nodded. 'Yes, I have heard. It doesn't do to listen to that sort of gossip, but one can't help wondering.'

'But it doesn't matter if you're not interested in him,' Martin said. 'I don't mind admitting that I'm quite relieved to hear you say that, Helen. Last night I had visions of being left out in the cold.'

'Well now you have the truth of the matter,' she replied, happy at having the opportunity of explaining. 'In any case, in my work I get only enough time to see one man!'

'And that man is me!' He smiled as he nodded. 'How are you getting on today? Almost finished?'

'Not yet. I've got another village to do yet. But I expect to get home around six.'

'And may I call about seven?'

'Please do.' Her eyes sparkled as she

told him, and he nodded slowly, reading her expression correctly.

'Thanks, Helen.' He reached out and squeezed her elbow. 'Now we'd better part. We're being watched from about seven different houses around here, and you know how people talk. Our reputations will suffer if we're not careful.'

'I don't think people are that malicious,' Helen replied with a smile. 'But I'll get on, anyway. See you this evening, Martin.'

'Without fail!' he replied . . .

8

For the next few days Helen found life favouring her. She saw nothing at all of Russell Thorpe, and as the days passed one after another the stresses departed from her mind. It all began to seem like some bad dream, the effects Russell had had on her. Now that it was past she could not help thinking it had all taken place only in her mind. No human being could command such mental power! It was incredible that she had ever believed Russell possessed it.

She saw quite a lot of Martin. He began calling around whenever he had the time, and at least every other evening saw him at the bungalow. Mrs Barclay took to him, and extended an invitation for him to join them on Sunday. Helen had to make a round in the morning, and would call upon only the more serious cases. She would be through long before lunch, and it was arranged that Martin would join them for lunch and remain until supper.

It was a beautiful morning when Helen left the bungalow. The sound of the local church bells came wafting across the meadow, filling the air with majestic tone. Helen had never felt so happy! Everything seemed to be working out for her! Fate had brought her here to this district, and directed Martin to the same place. There seemed nothing more to be said. Everything she hoped for seemed contained in the one small fact that Martin was interested in her.

She had a call to make at one of the council houses near Thorpe's Farm, and Helen slowed as she neared the meadow where the pond was. No matter the time of day she never forgot to check the pond for the presence of children, since that first day when she had met Russell. This morning she was appalled to see half a dozen youngsters throwing stones into the water and shouting and whooping around the pond. She stopped her car and alighted, intent upon giving the children a good dressing down. But as she went through the gate towards them she saw Russell himself coming across the meadow. The children spotted him almost in the same instant, and they came streaming towards the gate with him in hot pursuit.

Helen remained where she was, knowing that Russell had seen her. The children passed her by and kept going back to their homes. Russell came panting up, a good natured grin on his tanned face.

'Were you coming in to throw stones into the water?' he demanded jocularly.

'No, I was after the children,' she replied. 'I do think it's too bad of you, Russell, not doing anything about this pond. It's been a fortnight, and you see how the children are attracted to the spot. One of them will surely drown before very long.'

'It won't be the first time someone

has drowned in this district,' he replied tightly. 'No doubt you've heard about the other, Helen.'

'I have no time for gossip,' she replied. 'What can you do about this pond, Russell?'

'I'm not bound by law to do anything. It's on my land, and I've taken normal steps to keep trespassers out. That's all I'm required to do. Would you have me spend something like a hundred pounds just to relieve the parents of those children of their responsibilities? It's up to the parents, surely!'

'That's true, but because they fail to see the danger is no reason why you should shirk your moral obligation.'

'I strung barbed wire along the hedge, and within a week the little terrors had torn holes through it.' He sighed heavily. 'I can't do any more, Helen.'

'Well it's not my place to insist,' she replied, half turning away.

'Are you in a hurry?'

'As usual.' She nodded. 'I must be one of the most busiest women in the district. But how is Mrs Farrell doing?'

'She's back home from the hospital,' he said. 'She's no trouble.' He sighed. 'I wish you had to attend her.'

'She won't need attention until she has the plaster removed. Give her my regards, won't you?'

'I thought you and your mother might call on her,' he said. 'She'd appreciate it.'

'Perhaps tomorrow evening,' Helen said instantly. 'I'm sure Mother would want to see her. I'm sorry I didn't think of it before.'

'You're too busy to think of much outside your work,' he stated. 'But it's a good thing to have a nurse like you in the district. I wish we could get together again.'

'I'm sorry, but it's out of the question, Russell.'

'Because of the doctor!' He nodded slowly. 'You don't have to tell me.' He stared at her, and she at once became aware of the unrest creeping into her mind. She blinked her eyes and shrugged her shoulders.

'I really must go,' she said sharply. 'Will you excuse me?'

'Certainly!' He followed her to the gate, and closed it after she had departed. 'Cheerio!' he called after her, and Helen turned and lifted a hand to him. She glanced into her driving mirror as she pulled away, and saw that he was leaning over the gate and staring after her.

She sighed deeply as she went on. It had happened again. Her mind was reeling from the attack he had made upon her, and yet he hadn't batted an eyelid while he spoke to her. She felt as if she had received an electric shock. What did it mean? What had happened? How could he project his personality to such a degree?

The morning seemed slow in passing, and Helen began to check her watch frequently, wondering if Martin had arrived at the bungalow. Eventually she finished her round and turned for home most thankfully. Barring emergencies, she was through for the day, and she looked forward to spending the rest of the time in Martin's company.

His car was not outside the bungalow when she reached home, and a glance at her watch warned her that he was cutting it close. Had anything happened to him? The query started a train of worry through her. She went into the house and set down her case, calling to her mother, and Mrs Barclay came through from the kitchen, smiling a welcome.

'Martin called about half an hour ago, Helen. He'll be late. There was an accident as he left town. He wasn't involved, but he's doing what he can until the ambulance arrives, and he'll come along as soon as he can.'

'I hope it's not a bad crash,' Helen said with a frown. 'I'll go and change out of this uniform, Mother. I won't be long.'

She went to her room and sank down upon the bed. She had a slight headache, and wondered if it had anything to do with her meeting Russell earlier. She took some aspirin, then showered and changed into a cool dress. She felt much refreshed as she went to see if there was anything she could do to help her mother. But as she reached the kitchen she heard the doorbell.

'I'll get it, Mother,' she called, and her steps seemed to lighten as she hurried along the hall. She opened the door to Martin, and he smiled and gripped her hands for a moment.

'Sorry I'm late,' he apologized.

'That's all right. What about the accident?'

'It was nasty. I was just coming over the bridge out of Truston when some maniac overtook me. You know how the road twists at that point, just past the bridge? The fool passed me, and was still on the opposite side of the road as he went around the bend. There was a car coming my way, and the driver ran on to the verge to avoid the road hog. It was rather rough on the verge and the poor devil stuck his head through the windscreen. The road hog didn't stop.'

'That was awful. Was the driver badly hurt?'

'Cut about quite a lot! I did what I could for him, but he really needed hospital treatment and the surgeon's needle. I had to wait and talk to the police, but there was not much I could tell them. I was too busy watching that fool of a driver to see if he would get around the bend safely that I didn't note his number. I expect he'll get away with it. I described his car, but that won't be much help without the number. And some poor devil he's never met will be scarred for the rest of his life!'

'Come and have a drink. I expect you can do with one.' Helen took his hand and led him into the lounge. 'Whisky?' she asked, opening the cocktail cabinet.

'That'll do fine, please,' he replied, standing near the window and looking across the garden.

Helen poured the drink and took it to him, and he kissed her gently on the mouth before taking it.

'Thank you, Helen,' he said softly. 'You're an angel. How did you get along this morning?'

'No complications,' she replied with a smile. 'Now with a little luck we should be able able to relax for the rest of the day.'

'What shall we do?' he demanded. 'Do you feel like going for a drive to the beach?'

'That's an idea!' Her blue eyes glistened.

'I'm sure your mother would enjoy it,' he added. 'That is unless you've decided upon something else.'

'No. I thought I'd leave it to you.'

'Wise girl.' His brown eyes were thoughtful as he sipped his drink. 'But let's leave it to your mother, shall we?'

'We'll ask her. Lunch is almost ready. I'll go and see if there's anything I can do for her, shall I?'

'Yes, do. I'll take a look around your garden if I may. Give me a call when you want me.'

Helen nodded, pleased that he was

making himself at home. She walked with him to the door and put it on the latch. He went outside and she went into the kitchen. But Mrs Barclay had finished her preparations, and lunch was ready.

The meal was a complete success as far as Helen was concerned. She sat at Martin's side, revelling in his company, and they chatted pleasantly, with Mrs Barclay trying to learn something about him. Helen was aware that he kept watching her, as if trying to sum her up, but she didn't mind, for she was doing exactly the same thing about him!

In the afternoon they decided to drive to the seaside, and Martin took them to a small fishing village, where they left the car and walked to the cliffs. There were large numbers of people on the beach, for the day was warm and bright, with just a slight breeze coming in off the sea. A holiday camp was nearby, and most of the people came from there. But they found a spot among the dunes and sat down to enjoy the sunshine. Martin spread his car rug, and for the first time in what seemed to Helen to be months, she found the conditions right to relax.

At first they chatted lazily, but the sun was hot, and their sheltered spot had accumulated great heat. Helen drowsed, hearing Martin's voice as from a great distance. Then she heard no more, and slept until a gentle hand shook her shoulder. She opened her eyes slowly, wondering if it was yet time to get up and start her round. Then she saw Martin and her mother watching her, and she was startled to find they were on the beach.

'Well you're a nice one to bring out, I must say,' Martin told her in mock severe tones. 'You've been asleep all afternoon.'

'Oh no!' Helen glanced wildly at her watch. 'I haven't.' She had some trouble focusing upon the dial, but when her eyes became accustomed to the brightness she saw the time was almost four. 'Good heavens!' she exclaimed. 'Why on earth did you let me sleep that long?'

'Because it was doing you good, dear,' Mrs Barclay's eyes were twinkling. 'Martin and I have been talking all afternoon, but now it's time to go home to tea.'

'I hope you've enjoyed your afternoon by the seaside,' Martin said with a grin.

'I've never done a thing like that before,' Helen said, shaking her head. 'I must be getting old to nod off like a grandmother.'

'Never mind, there'll be other times to come down here,' Martin told her. 'The summer hasn't started yet.'

They drove back home, and Helen sat beside Martin, her head still thick with sleep. She had slept a little too soundly, and the afternoon seemed too bright for her eyes. But she was filled with a sense of wellbeing, and there was none of the strain left in her mind.

After tea Mrs Barclay insisted that they went for a drive alone. She excused herself on the grounds of having taken too much sun in the afternoon, and Helen suggested that they stay at home, but her mother was adamant.

'You young people need to get away together,' she said. 'Now off you go and don't argue about it.'

'I shall think you don't want to go with me,' Martin said, 'if you keep trying to find reasons why we should stay here.'

'Come along then. I'm ready to go,' Helen said instantly.

'But I'll take you on one condition,' Martin said firmly.

'What's that?' she demanded.

'You won't fall asleep in the car.'

'I promise.' Helen kissed her mother's cheek and they departed. 'We won't be late,' she said.

'Go and enjoy yourselves,' Mrs Barclay told them, accompanying them to the door.

'We will,' Helen said.

Martin was humming to himself as

they drove along the lane, and when they reached the main road he glanced at her.

'Where would you like to go?' he asked.

'Anywhere. You're driving. Just go on and on all evening.'

'You wouldn't like to stop anywhere for part of the time?' he queried, and there was a faint smile upon his lips.

'Yes, I would,' she retorted. 'It's been some time, hasn't it, since the last time?'

'Far too long. That spot on the beach would have been ideal.'

'I am sorry about this afternoon. Whatever must you think of me, Martin?'

'You really want me to tell you now?' he countered.

'If it's as exciting as your tones suggest then yes,' she replied. 'I dare you!'

'You've a lot to learn about me yet, Helen, and one of the things that will show itself before long is my inability to resist a dare. So you want to know what I think of you!' He shook his head. 'I'd better not say because it might upset your ego. You'd get a swelled head and then I'd be able to do nothing with you.'

'You're teasing me!'

'I wouldn't dream of it.' He shook his head. 'If you really want to know then you'll have to wait until I park the car. I can't talk on such deep matters while driving. My concentration has to be on the road.'

'Then stop the car now, in a gateway, and tell me,' Helen commanded.

'Now you're getting impatient, and your medical training should have removed that weakness from your character,' he said. 'We'll go on, Helen, to a spot I want to show you. I haven't been there since I was a boy, and I'd like to see it again.'

'Where is it?' she demanded eagerly. 'You know such nice places, Martin.'

'It isn't that so much,' he retorted. 'The fact is, you like the same things I do. We're very much two of a kind, Helen.'

'Do you think so?' Her eyes sparkled as she stared at him, and the smile on her lips put a curve into her cheeks. He stared at her for a moment, his own eyes glinting, and Helen felt the impulse to reach out and touch him. She was falling in love with him!

'I don't think so,' he retorted. 'I know for certain.'

They were silent for a bit, and Helen gazed around as he drove along unfrequented lanes that only one with local knowledge would know. The evening was perfect, and with the windows rolled down Helen could hear the birds singing and smell the freshness of the countryside.

Presently they joined a wider road, and she saw a signpost that indicated they were approaching a ferry. But Martin stopped the car in a gateway. They alighted, and he pointed out the earthworks that formed the river bank, winding across the marshes. Here and there were the tall white and blue sails of slowly moving yachts, looking for all the world as if they were drifting across the marshes. Cattle were grazing in small groups across the wide spread of flat land, and Helen could hear ducks quacking on a nearby pond.

'You slept all afternoon so you won't be tired for a stroll along the river bank,' Martin said cheerfully. 'Some exercise will do you good. You drive around in your car all week, when you ought to be on a bicycle, thinking of your figure.' He was smiling as he spoke, and Helen caught his mood.

'I'll match you stride for stride anywhere you want to go,' she said bravely, and he looked down at her shoes.

'At least they're sensible,' he remarked. 'Come along. We'll go along the river bank as far as that road bridge. Can you see it in the distance? We crossed it this afternoon on our way to the beach.'

'I see it.' Helen's blue eyes picked out the arc of concrete that carried the distant road across the river. 'But that must be all of five miles away.'

'Coward!' He laughed heartily. 'As a matter of fact it's nearer three, and we won't go all the way. We'll come back on the footpath across the marshes.'

'Are there any bulls among those cattle out there?' she demanded as they walked towards the river.

'Perhaps, but I'm country-born, remember, and I won't do anything foolish. You're perfectly safe in my hands, Helen.'

'I'm sure I am,' she retorted, and their glances met and he took her hand.

It was more than pleasant to stroll along the river bank, holding hands, without a care in the world. They watched the holidaymakers enjoying themselves in the pleasure craft that formed busy traffic on the quiet waterway. Yachts sailed majestically by, heeling first to one side and then the other under the pull of breeze and sails. It was all so new to Helen that she felt captivated by the sights. There were swans along the banks, perfectly white, with black markings around their beaks, and scores of ducks diving and feeding and squabbling over titbits thrown from passing craft.

'How far have we walked?' Helen demanded when they had been strolling for an hour.

'About a mile and a half, I'd say.' Martin narrowed his eyes as he turned first in one direction and then another to get his bearings. 'Done enough, do you think?'

'For the moment.' Her pale blue eyes were bright as she stared up at him. 'Let's find a nice spot down there on the marshes and sit down to rest. Then you can tell me all about what you think of me.'

'All right.' There was an answering smile upon his face. 'We'll have to walk to that gateway before we can get on to the marshes. You have to know your way around this place or you'll find that you have to keep jumping ditches to get anywhere.'

Helen stared across the stretch of rich green grazing land, and saw that it was closely intersected by ditches. It was silent, reminding her of a frozen tableau, with the cattle grouped about and hardly moving as they grazed. A flight of birds sped overhead, circled, then dropped down out of sight in the grass. The faint breeze held a strange smell, a mixture of earth and grass that mingled in her nostrils and filled her with a sense of awareness of Nature. She breathed deeply, moved by the solitude of the place, and Martin smiled, for he knew all about it.

They walked on to the marshes, their feet sinking into the rich turf. A nearby group of cows lifted their black and white heads and stared curiously at them. Helen took Martin's hand, and put him between them and herself, and he laughed.

'They won't hurt you, Helen,' he said. 'If you waved your arms they'd turn tail and flee.'

'Perhaps they can sense that I'm nervous of them,' she replied.

'Come along. I'll show you a spot where I once took a pike weighing six and a half pounds.'

'Do you like fishing and things like

that?' she demanded

'I used to, but I haven't the time to follow my boyish pursuits since I became a doctor.'

'Don't you think it a pity that one has to grow up?'

He smiled as he looked down at her. 'Do you think I'd make a good Peter Pan?' he countered.

'I didn't mean that exactly,' she replied. 'I think it's a pity we lose the ability to see magic in small things such as this scene. I never knew such places existed. Just for the sake of sparing an hour or so, I've discovered something. I'm not going to let life drag me on from day to day in future, Martin. I'm going to make time for relaxing.'

'I'm glad to hear you saying so,' he told her. 'We'll find the time together, shall we?'

'Yes.' She nodded, and when she glanced at him their gazes held. He tightened his grip on her hand, and took hold of her around the waist. His eyes narrowed a little, as if the sun was too bright for him, and Helen studied his handsome face, taking in every detail that she was getting to know so well.

'I think this is the right time and place to tell you what I think of you, Helen,' he said slowly. 'I was attracted to you from the very first moment, but the past few days have been more important. I've never been in love before, and I'm not sure I know what it is. But lately I've been feeling restless, and when I'm not with you I want to rush through my work and come out to see you. I find a strange sort of peace when I'm in your company. Take this evening for example. I wish time would stand still and keep us here like this forever.'

His voice trembled a little as he spoke, and Helen felt a rush of joy inside her. His arms tightened about her and he lowered his head towards her, his mouth coming gently against hers. She shivered as their lips touched, and then emotion seized her and she flung her arms-about his neck, clinging to him as if her very life depended upon their closeness.

It was like being splashed with enchantment, Helen thought remotely. Her eyes were closed and she swayed in his embrace. All her feelings were running riot, and she didn't have a coherent thought in her mind. Now time seemed to stand still, and she wished it would never start up again. But she could hear the ticking of Martin's wristwatch, and reality stayed in the background to keep a rein upon her.

When he released her, his face was flushed, and Helen knew hers would be similarly painted. She could see herself in the brightness of his eyes, and her joy knew no bounds. She was trembling inside, dominated by strong feelings that swept through her like a tidal wave.

'I love you, Helen,' he said huskily, his face close to hers. 'I do love you, even though I haven't any idea what being in love feels like.'

'Martin.' His name trembled upon her lips. 'I feel it, too, deep inside I can't explain it fully. It's so strange and wonderful. But I'm very happy that I came here as the district nurse. I have the feeling that we were meant to meet.'

'And to fall in love?' He nodded as he smiled. 'That's what I call the hand of Fate. Helen, time is young yet, I know, but I have to tell you I love you. If you know about it then there's a chance that you'll feel the same way about me. In any case, if you know, there can't be any misunderstanding between us. I'm not ashamed of what I feel for you. I don't have to get to know you any better to add to what I've already learned about you. You're the dearest and sweetest girl in the world. Whenever I've thought of having a wife there's been a cloudy picture in my mind of my dream girl. Her face never really came into focus, but if I could have seen her I'm sure she would have had your face.'

'We have plenty of time to get to

know each other,' she replied slowly. 'I've never met anyone quite like you, Martin. You seem to have exactly the same interests I do. You're a romantic, and so am I. You're sentimental, because you've come back here to work where you spent your life as a boy. That's what I like about you.'

'Then we're agreed that at least we like one another,' he said with a smile. 'I'm quite prepared to start building on that basis, Helen. But what about you, Helen?'

'Yes.' She nodded. 'I know what you mean, and I agree. I think we're going to find life very interesting in future, don't you?'

'And happy!' He took her arm and they began to walk on across the marshes, alone and wrapped up in each other. The sun was setting by the time they turned back to the car, and the crimson and scarlet glow that filled the western sky seemed to be a good omen, to Helen's happy way of thinking.

9

Monday mornings had never seemed blue to Helen, but when she awoke the next morning she felt on top of the World. She arose quickly and soon prepared for the day's round. At breakfast her mother remarked upon her high spirits, and Helen smiled to herself, not ready to divulge what lay uppermost in her mind. But she came down a degree or two when the telephone rang as she was preparing to leave. Russell Thorpe had given up ringing during the past day or two, causing Helen to think that he was beginning to get the message that they were not meant for each other. Becoming engrossed with Martin had released her from the pressures that Russell seemed to put into her mind, and she felt that she was beyond the pull of that strange power of his. But she didn't want to answer the phone in case it was Russell at the other end of the line.

Mrs Barclay came from the kitchen to answer the instrument's shrill insistence for attention, and Helen's heart seemed to sink when her mother mentioned Russell's name.

'Of course, Russell. I'll call this afternoon. I'll get Helen to drive me over when she sets out again after lunch. No, she's not here now. She left about five minutes ago.'

When her mother hung up Helen turned to take up her case.

'I've promised to go visit Mrs Farrell this afternoon, Helen,' Mrs Barclay said. 'Will you drive me there on your way out after lunch, and pick me up later?'

'Yes, Mother. I'm sorry, but I forgot to mention it yesterday. I saw Russell and he did say something about visiting Mrs Farrell.'

'I would have gone before but I just didn't think of it,' her mother replied.

'But at least you won't be able to stop, so don't worry about seeing too much of Russell.'

'You've taken a dislike to him, Mother!' Helen accused.

'Not as such,' Mrs Barclay replied. 'I've said before that there is something about him I don't like. But it's an uneasiness rather than pure dislike. And those wicked stories that are going around about him don't help at all.'

'I don't pay them any heed, but that doesn't make any difference as far as I'm concerned,' Helen said slowly. 'There is something very strange about him, and when I spend any amount of time in his company I can feel it quite plainly.'

'Perhaps that's why he's never married.' Mrs Barclay shook her head slowly. 'He might have that kind of personality which repels'

'I don't think it's that either,' Helen replied, thinking about it. 'He attracts rather than repels, but he seems to dominate one. I've never experienced it before. But when I begin to feel his power I get shadows of evil in my mind.'

'Poor Helen! Is that how he affected you that Sunday we went to tea?'

'Not at the time. It seemed to fill my mind afterwards.' Helen suppressed a shudder and went to the door. 'I'll be home at the usual time, Mother,' she said. 'Goodbye.'

'Be careful, dear,' her mother responded.

Helen was thoughtful as she drove around the villages that morning, attending the patients. There was a sombre note in her mind that did much to flatten the high feelings of romance that surrounded Martin and thoughts of him. Why did the mere mention of Russell Thorpe send shivers along her spine? She shook her head slowly, convinced that there was something seriously wrong about Russell that didn't show.

She saw Martin later that morning, and they stood on the roadside and chatted, touching upon their feelings and the pleasant time they'd spent the previous evening. Martin held her hands, and Helen could see his emotions showing plainly in his dark brown eyes.

'I've been so impatient to see you this morning, Helen,' he said. 'You look wonderful. How are you?'

'Getting along fine. I've got Spring fever, I think. I got up in a wonderful frame of mind this morning.'

'Dare I hope that it came from knowing me?' he asked cautiously, and she smiled as she nodded emphatically.

'There's no one else,' she said cheerfully. 'There's only you, Martin.'

'That's what I want to hear.' He sighed deeply as he glanced at his watch. 'May I come and see you this evening, Helen, or do you think it's becoming too much of a good thing?'

'No! Don't say that, Martin. Come by all means. I find the time dragging in between our meetings. You're not the only one with feelings, you know.'

He kissed her quickly, looking around worriedly as he did so. Helen laughed vibrantly.

'Still worried about your reputation?' she teased.

'We can't be too careful at this early stage,' he said. 'But now you'd better go, Helen, before your presence tempts me again. I'll see you this evening, sweetheart.'

She smiled at him as they parted, going in opposite directions. Helen could feel a bubbling sensation in her breast. It would not be controlled or contained. This was love, she knew, and the knowledge sent deeper pangs right through her. Life had suddenly opened up for her. The close horizons had lifted, and now the sky seemed to be the limit. It was all so uplifting and exciting, and her hands trembled upon the steering wheel. It was amazing that a man could suddenly become so important to a girl.

After lunch she drove her mother to Thorpe's Farm, and felt tension creep up inside her as they approached the place. Was she feeling guilty about the way she had allowed Russell to kiss her on their first visit here? She shook her head emphatically, forgetting her mother's presence as she drew in before the large farmhouse. She hadn't allowed him to kiss her. She had been the victim of that strange power of his, unable to prevent him filling her with strange and powerful impulses.

'I won't stay at all, Mother,' Helen said as she switched off the engine. 'I must get on with my round. But I'd better just pop in to speak to Mrs Farrell.'

'And you can call for me when you're through for the day,' her mother said as they got out of the car. 'Don't worry about the time, dear.'

'All right.' Helen smiled, but her steps lagged as they walked towards the house. She saw the door opening, and her heart almost missed a beat when Russell appeared, smiling widely in welcome.

'I'm so glad you could come,' he said. 'Poor Mrs Farrell is finding the time heavy upon her. She's always been such an active woman.'

'I should think she has,' Helen said quickly. 'She's taken care of this place on her own for years, hasn't she?'

'Only because she wouldn't have another woman in the house,' he replied. 'But there's nothing she can do about it now. I've got one of the local women in to do the cleaning while Mrs Farrell is off her feet.'

They went into the house, and Helen fought off the sensation of being stifled. She was aware that Russell was watching her closely, but with such sweet thoughts of Martin in front of her mind she did not fear his mental attentions now.

Mrs Farrell was not cheerful when they entered her room, but she brightened when she saw them. Russell did not stay, and Helen glanced towards the door as he closed it. She could not help sighing as his presence seemed to flow from the room after him. She greeted Mrs Farrell, and then began to think of leaving, but the old housekeeper reached out a shaking hand and took hold of Helen.

'I want to talk to you, Helen,' she said. 'I know you're very busy. Even now you're thinking of getting back to your patients. But spare me a few moments.'

'All right,' Helen said, smiling. 'What can I do for you, Mrs Farrell?'

'I want to talk to you about Russell. He's such a lonely man, and when you first came here you seemed so friendly towards him.' Mrs Farrell paused and watched Helen's face for reaction.

'I'm still friendly towards him, Mrs Farrell,' Helen said stiffly. 'But I'm a very busy woman, you know.'

'That isn't exactly what I mean. I know you're friendly, but you don't like him, do you?'

'I do. I think he's a personable man.'

'I was afraid you'd heard those wicked stories about him! They're enough to put anyone off. But they're not true, Helen, I assure you. Poor Russell is quite upset that you may believe them.'

Helen made no reply, and Mrs Barclay glanced at her. 'Isn't it time you went on your way, Helen? I know you're pressed for time. I'll stay and keep Mrs Farrell company until you return for me.'

'Yes, I really must go, Mrs Farrell.' Helen made an effort to speak normally. 'I'm so glad to see you making obvious strides towards recovery. You'll be out of that plaster in no time at all, and you'll be able to get around again as you've always done. You're a very good patient, by all accounts.'

'I'll see you again, shan't I? 'the old lady demanded eagerly.

'Yes, I'll call and see you again,' Helen said. 'Goodbye for now.'

She smiled at her mother and went to the door, and her hands trembled as she opened it and went out to the landing. Where was Russell? Had he gone off about his business or was he waiting around somewhere to see her when she departed? She went down the wide stairs and breathed deeply in relief when she gained the outside without seeing him. But as she reached her car his voice called to her, loud and insistent.

'Helen, don't go for a moment. I want to talk to you.'

She turned to see him coming across the yard, and the smile on his face reminded her of a picture she had seen as a child of the wolf accosting Little Red Riding Hood in the woods. She drew a sharp breath and made an effort to set her resistance into action. He came close to her, standing over her, his heavy body showing muscular strength.

'I'm in a dreadful hurry now, Russell,' she said.

'I shan't keep you more than a few moments,' he replied softly, in a commanding tone. 'I want to ask you a question.'

'Yes?' She snapped the word at him, and saw a smile come to his face. He was handsome and attractive, she thought remotely, and could not help wondering why he hadn't found himself a wife.

'I want to take you out one evening. We've known each other for some time now, and we haven't been out together. You're doing pretty well with that doctor friend of yours, but I think you'd enjoy yourself with me just as much.'

She started to protest that her time was limited, but he stopped her with a gesture.

'I know you're a busy girl,' he said. 'But you do get some free time. You had a good day yesterday, didn't you?'

'What do you mean?' she demanded.

'You went down to the beach in the afternoon, and in the evening you were on the marshes by the ferry.'

'How do you know?' Helen couldn't keep surprise out of her voice. She saw him smile, but there was no expression in his eyes, only a tense alertness.

'You'll soon find that you can't do anything around the villages without someone knowing about it,' he retorted. 'Country people never needed the telephone, you know. Now what about us getting together?'

Again Helen could feel the mysterious pull of his mind against hers, and she stiffened against it. She shook her head.

'No, Russell, thank you,' she said tremulously. 'It isn't that I dislike you. But I just don't want to.'

His face set a little into harsh lines, and his eyes seemed to fill with ice. Helen watched him for a moment, filled with a dread that seemed to send icy shivers along her spine. The silence of the yard seemed to close in about her like a ghost preparing to scare some nervous mortal. She breathed heavily and let the breath go in a sigh.

'Now I must go, Russell,' she said. 'I'm sorry if I've hurt you in any way, but it's only right that I should tell you exactly what's in my mind.'

'You don't know your own mind,' he said thinly, and a smile flitted across his sharp face. 'Look at me and I'll prove it to you. Look into my eyes, Helen.'

There was a strangely compelling note in his voice, and Helen looked into his eyes despite herself. She immediately felt the power of his mind, and tried to break it. But she felt so helpless before him. It was as if her will power was draining away, and she felt inert and incredibly weary.

'Helen, I want to see you this evening, here at the farm,' he said quietly, insistently. 'When you've finished your duties you can come here to me.'

'No,' she said. 'Martin is coming to see me.' She spoke unwillingly, yet there was a strange urge deep inside her to tell him the truth. She felt that she wanted him to know of the happiness that Martin was bringing into her life. She didn't realize that it was Russell's strange power that made her want to tell him.

'So it is that doctor, eh?' he demanded. 'I thought as much. He had that look about him when he came to see Mrs Farrell. But I've been too busy myself to worry about anything else. If I hadn't been you would be my girl now, Helen.'

'No.' She shook her head. 'It'll never come to that, Russell.' She found that the mention of Martin's name broke the spell somewhat, and she blinked her eyes and stirred in the hot sunlight, feeling for all the world as if she were just awakening from a deep sleep. 'You're wasting your time if you're waiting for me to fall in love with you, Russell. I'm not the type of girl to love two men at the same time.'

'Are you in love with him?' A harsh note sounded in his voice. 'Has it gone as far as that?'

'It has. Perhaps now you'll leave me alone.' Helen turned away, but he reached out and caught hold of her arm. 'Please, Russell, don't,' she said quickly. 'You're wasting your time.'

'A man would be a fool not to waste a little time trying to get you,' he retorted. 'How can you know that you're in love with him? You haven't known him all that long.' He shook his head in disbelief. 'I think his smooth ways have turned your head, Helen. You knew me before you met him. Give me a chance.'

His gaze was hypnotic, and Helen realized it as she stared into his dark eyes. She felt herself slipping again, losing her control, and although she fought against it there seemed little she could do about it. The only safe way to remain out of his clutches was to stay well away from him, she thought remotely, and tried to strengthen her intentions to do so. She wouldn't even bring her mother here again.

'I must go, Russell!' The call of her duty was strong inside her, and Helen found the effort to break through his power. She dropped her gaze from his. 'Let me go,' she said firmly.

'I'm not stopping you.' He smiled thinly. 'I wouldn't dream of stopping you. If you ever come to me it will be of your own free will.'

She got into the car, glad to be able to sit down because her legs were trembling. She felt hot and uneasy as she started the car, and her eyes ached as if she had been staring too long at the sun. Now she avoided his gaze, and turned the car and drove swiftly away. As she left the farm a great sigh of relief escaped her.

But she had the answer to his power now! He must be skilled in hypnotism, either consciously or otherwise, and he was using his persuasiveness against her. He had begun it from the very first moment they met, she realized with a start, and she vowed never to meet him again unless she had someone with her. That would be the only way to avoid trouble. She shuddered as intangible impulses throbbed through her mind. What had he been thinking while he worked his power against her? She recalled the intensity of his gaze, and felt as if hot water had been poured over her.

As the afternoon went on Helen slowly recovered from her meeting with Russell, and she felt drained of her strength, as if she were recovering from an illness. She didn't wonder that the local girl who had drowned herself had got into such a state over Russell! Now she felt she knew why! But had Russell deliberately led the girl into performing such a tragic act? Is that what the local people meant when they said Russell was more than responsible for the girl's death? Helen had automatically suspected that they meant Russell had actually pushed her into the water, but now she was certain he wouldn't have to go that far to achieve his ends. The power of his mind was overwhelming.

She determined to tell Martin about it when she saw him. For some reason she felt that Russell might try to cause a breach between them. She didn't know where the thought came from, but it was there in the forefront of her mind. She found, as the afternoon progressed, that other strange thoughts were forming in her brain. She went on with her work instinctively, not needing to concentrate fully upon what she was doing. But towards the end of the afternoon she was filled with strange impulses which were entirely out of character.

She couldn't put anything into shape

because the impressions remained firmly embedded in her subconscious mind, but she was aware of them and realized that they troubled her, whatever they were. Was this some more of Russell's doing? She shook her head as she considered it. She couldn't accept that. Nothing he tried to do would have the slightest effect upon her. She was too occupied with Martin to care about anything else, and she knew that not all people made good subjects for hypnotism. It was common knowledge that anyone with any will power at all could resist the skill of the hypnotist.

That thought seemed to calm her a little, and when she finished the round she started back to Thorpe Farm to collect her mother. She didn't like the idea of going there, but she steeled herself for the ordeal, determining not to allow herself to see Russell alone. Her mother would be with her and that would count for much.

Parking the car in front of the house, Helen alighted and went to the door.

She was tensing more and more as she walked along the stone path, and at any moment she expected Russell to pop up like some bad fairy. But he didn't even come to the door as usual. Helen had to knock, and some moments elapsed before the door was opened by a strange, oldish woman.

'Oh, hello, Nurse,' the woman greeted. 'Come in, won't you? Mrs Barclay told me you'd be calling soon. You know your way up to Mrs Farrell's room, don't you?'

'Yes thank you,' Helen said. 'You're helping Mr Thorpe out while Mrs Farrell is laid up, aren't you?'

'That's right, Nurse. You won't know me, but I live next door to a patient of yours. I've often seen you call. I'm Mrs Dagleish.'

'I'm pleased to meet you, Mrs Dagleish, but don't you find taking care of this large house too much for one woman?'

'There's a lot to it, but if Mrs Farrell can cope normally then I'm sure I can manage,' came the smiling reply. 'You know the old lady won't have a maid in the house.'

'Why? She isn't afraid some younger woman might come along and take her job away from her, is she?'

'No, it isn't that.' The woman lowered her voice as she closed the front door. 'A maid wouldn't come into this house if she had any sense.'

'Now you're talking as if there is some truth in those nasty rumours, Mrs Dagleish,' Helen said firmly.

'No.' The woman shook her head. 'You weren't here when that happened! There was quite a to-do, I can tell you. There was more to it than meets the eye, Nurse.'

'Where is Mr Thorpe? He wouldn't like to hear you saying this sort of thing.'

'He went off in his car about half an hour ago,' Mrs Dagleish said. 'I don't mind telling you that I thought twice about coming in to work. It was partly for Mrs Farrell's sake that I agreed to, I don't mind telling you. And I'm past my best now. I don't think anything is likely to happen to me.'

Helen didn't laugh, and the woman sobered and nodded.

'I'll go and fetch my mother,' Helen said. 'I have to get back home as soon as possible in case there are any emergency calls.'

'Well you know the way,' came the pert reply, and Helen started up the stairs. She wanted to get out of the house before Russell came back. There was a jumpy feeling inside her, and it wouldn't go until they were clear of the place.

Mrs Farrell was a great deal more cheerful when Helen looked in upon her, and Mrs Barclay got to her feet from a chair beside the bed.

'Here's Helen back, Mrs Farrell, so it's time I must go. But I'll come and see you again. We have had a nice chat, haven't we?'

'It's made a nice change,' the old housekeeper said, and Helen wondered how much the woman knew about her employer. Did she know more than the average villager about what had happened to that girl? 'You'll come and see me, Helen, won't you?' Mrs Farrell was ready to begin again where she had left off at Helen's departure earlier that afternoon.

'When I get time,' Helen promised.

'Where is Russell then? He hasn't been up here once this afternoon to see me.'

'Mrs Dagleish tells me he left the house and went off in his car about half an hour ago.' Helen caught her mother's eye and nodded. It was time to go.

'That woman! I don't like her prowling around.' Mrs Farrell shook her head vehemently. 'She can't do half the work I get through, and what she does isn't finished off by any means.'

'Well I'll come and see you again,' Mrs Barclay said, patting the old housekeeper's hand. 'Goodbye for now.'

'Goodbye. You've been very kind to an old woman.' Mrs Farrell watched Helen closely as she and her mother departed, and Helen sighed with relief as they left the house.

'How did it go, Mother?' she asked when they were driving away from the farm.

'A pleasant enough afternoon, but have you noticed the overpowering atmosphere in the house? It came to me as I was sitting there. And I do declare that Russell prowled up and down those stairs a hundred times during the afternoon. I heard his footsteps passing the door over and over again. It began to get on my nerves.'

'Never mind. Mrs Farrell will soon be on her feet again, and then she'll be too busy putting the house back into the way she likes it to worry about having visitors. You've done your good deed, Mother.'

'I've never spoken seriously to you about your activities, Helen, but I feel I ought to warn you not to visit Russell Thorpe there at the house.'

'Mother, whatever do you mean?' Helen was startled by the deep tone of her mother's voice, and she glanced sideways in time to see a worried expression flit across the older woman's face.

'That's just it, I don't know what I mean. All I can tell you is that I don't like the thought of you going there alone, Helen.'

'Well don't worry about that because I haven't the slightest desire to do so.' Helen smiled thinly. 'No doubt Martin would have something to say if I did.'

They went home, and Helen was glad to get out of her uniform. She took a shower, and stood under the pelting stream of water, feeling it knocking the weariness out of her but realizing that it couldn't cleanse her mind. She felt a little as if she were suffering mental shock, and when she recalled that afternoon with Russell she could not prevent horror flitting through her. What did it all add up to? What was in Russell's intent and powerful mind? What did he want with her? Helen didn't know, and the unknown seemed to hold terror for some unaccountable reason.

But Martin would soon be arriving! That thought cheered her up and she hurriedly dressed for the evening. She heard the telephone ring as she was making up, and wondered if it could be a call for her services as a nurse. The next moment her mother tapped at the door, and popped her head around it.

'Helen, that was Martin!' Mrs Barclay said hurriedly. 'He won't be able to come here this evening. He's had an accident with his car.'

'What?' Helen leapt to her feet in fear. 'Is he all right, Mother?'

'He says he is. It seems he lost control as he pulled out of his driveway. There's something wrong with his steering. He's got a mechanic there now, looking it over, and he said if you had nothing to do perhaps you'd run into Truston to see him.'

'I'll go,' Helen said 'Did he hang up?'

'Yes. He wants to see what the mechanic is doing. But you can go and see him, Helen'

'I'm on my way.' Helen checked her

face in the mirror, then took her handbag. 'I don't think there'll be any calls for me, Mother, but I'll ring in about half an hour, just in case. I'll see you later.'

'I hope you'll find that everything is all right, Helen,' Mrs Barclay called after her.

Helen silently agreed as she went out to her car, and she drove fast along the lane, her mind filled with conflicting thoughts. But as long as Martin was unharmed it didn't matter about his car. That could always be fixed.

She stopped at the garage on the main road to have the tank filled, and then she went on towards Truston, seven miles away. She drove fast, intent upon reaching Martin as soon as possible, but a large car swept past her at terrific speed on a short straight, then slowed in front, its brake lights flickering. Helen frowned as she slowed, thinking that someone from the village had recognized her and wanted her services. She pulled on the verge, glad that she made a habit of always having her case along with her. Then she saw the man getting out of the big car, and her heart missed a beat. It was Russell Thorpe, and he was grinning tensely as he came towards her!

10

'Russell, you always turn up when I'm in a flaming hurry,' Helen got in before he could speak.

'I thought you were travelling fast,' he retorted. 'But I have to talk to you, Helen. It is rather urgent.'

'What's on your mind?' she demanded.

'Not here. We can cut down the side road about a hundred yards along there and go to my farm.'

'I haven't the time for that. I told you I'm in a hurry. But what is it that you can't talk about here? Russell, I'll tell you for the last time that you're making a mistake by thinking I shall get interested in you. We're not meant for each other.'

'How do you know?' he countered. 'You haven't given us a chance.'

'Because I know without having to try it.'

'You didn't feel like that on the Sunday you came to mine to tea,' he retorted. 'I don't think Reade would like to know about that.'

Helen stared at him for some moments, waiting for him to go on, but he was expressionless, his lips thin in his face. She sighed. 'Are you trying to blackmail me into seeing you?' she demanded. 'What's wrong with you, Russell? You're an attractive, handsome man, and yet you haven't a girl friend? Is there something in your past that I don't know about?'

'You know very well what's in my past,' he replied angrily. 'I think it's those malicious tongues that have scared you off.'

'Nonsense! I don't listen to gossip.'

'You changed after that Sunday. It was the next day when that doctor started around here. It won't last with him, you know.'

'I don't know what you're talking about, and if this is all you have stopped me for then I'm displeased about it,'

Helen told him furiously. 'Move your car out of the way and I'll go on.'

'Not until you've promised to see me on one of your free evenings,' he said firmly.

'Don't take this too far, Russell. I'm losing my patience. I've already told you I'm in a hurry.'

'I'll have a talk with Reade. Perhaps I can get through to him.'

'I shall talk to him myself,' Helen snapped, losing her temper. 'You won't have to bother telling him about that Sunday evening. I will take great pleasure in saving you the trouble.'

There was a silence between them, and Helen could feel her courage slipping away. There was an intentness in Russell's eyes that frightened her. She was beginning to wonder what was in his mind when she heard the sound of a motor scooter behind. Turning quickly, she saw with overwhelming relief the local policeman coming along. She hadn't seen him but once or twice, and always at a distance, since meeting him on the road on her first day in the village, but now he was arriving as if he had been sent for, and such was her relief that she turned to Russell, who was staring morosely at the newcomer.

'If you don't go then I'll complain to him that you're pestering me,' she said.

'I'm going, but I'll see you later,' he replied.

The policeman was slowing, and he pulled in beside Helen, smiling as he removed his crash helmet. 'Are you in trouble?' he demanded.

'No, thank you, Constable. Everything's under control. Mr Thorpe was just leaving.'

'Cheerio then,' Russell said, and turned away. He went to his car, got in hurriedly and drove away fast.

Helen sighed inaudibly as she watched him go, and when she looked at the policeman she saw that he was watching her gravely. 'Is anything wrong?' she demanded.

'I advise you to tell me if there is, Nurse,' he retorted. 'That man isn't one to fool around with.'

'I'm afraid I don't understand, Constable.'

'Then perhaps I ought to make you understand.' He got off his scooter and propped it on its stand. He was tall and powerful, towering above her, and his brown eyes were filled with concern. 'I haven't seen much of you around the villages,' he said slowly. 'But I've been hearing a lot about your work. You're doing great things by all accounts, Nurse. It would be a pity if you got mixed up with a man like Russell Thorpe.'

'I've been hearing stories about him,' Helen said slowly. 'I never pay much heed to rumours and gossip, but I don't mind admitting that Russell Thorpe makes me nervous. I have no interest in him, if that's what you're thinking. He was pestering me just now, although I wouldn't go so far as to make an official complaint.'

'Quite.' He nodded slowly. 'It wouldn't do to have stories like that going the rounds. But I don't mind telling you that I've got an eye on Thorpe, Nurse.'

'Has he done anything wrong, Constable? Is he likely to do anything wrong?' Helen could feel tension building up inside her.

'Part of my job is crime prevention,' came the smooth reply. He laughed harshly. 'There isn't much crime in these peaceful villages, not like you get in the towns, but we get our share, you know. You've heard those stories about Thorpe, you say. Well I don't know if there is any truth in them. If there was then Thorpe would be behind bars now. But I do know he was responsible for that girl's death, although he never pushed her into the river as some people say. He's not to be trusted around women, Nurse, and seeing you with him makes me see to it that you know.'

'I have no interest in him,' Helen said 'To tell you the truth I'm a little scared of him.'

'And you may have a perfect right to be,' came the grave reply. 'There's always been a cloud over Russell Thorpe. He's pestering you now, you say?'

'He stopped me just now, and he was talking to me in the same vein earlier this afternoon,' Helen said reluctantly. 'But I don't want to put the matter into your hands, Constable. If anything is said it might make the situation more difficult.'

'That's true, but on the other hand you do get called out in the middle of the night sometimes, and I wouldn't want to get a call myself, to find you lying in the hedge somewhere.'

'Oh Lord! It isn't as bad as that, is it?' she demanded.

'I don't want to frighten you, Nurse, but that is my personal opinion. I've been watching Thorpe for a long time, and my task is made easier by the fact that none of the local girls will let him within a mile of them. I'm glad you know about him. But be very careful when you're travelling alone and late at night. If he does bother you again then don't hesitate to let me know. I'll soon put him off.'

'Thank you, but I hope it won't ever

come to that.' Helen frowned as she stared along the road. 'What is the trouble with him then? He doesn't appear mentally deficient to me.'

'I don't know myself, but you can take it from me that something is wrong.' There was a deadly serious note in the policeman's voice. 'That poor girl who drowned herself was in some state just before she did it. But there was no proof against Thorpe in any way.'

'I see.' Helen recalled the strange power that Russell Thorpe could emanate, and she breathed deeply to release some of the tension growing inside her. 'Then I'll keep in touch with you, Constable, if I may.'

'Please do, and let me know if he bothers you again. It won't go any further than me, I promise you, and I might be able to scare him off. But talking of your night calls. You don't get all that many of them, and perhaps it would be a good thing if you gave me a ring any time you have to go out. If I'm not at home I can always get a message.

My wife calls the police station in Truston and they put through a call to me on the radio.' He indicated his scooter, and smiled. 'We're well up to date in these parts now. There's a radio on there. If I know you're out, and where you're going, I can always keep an eye on you.'

'Thank you.' Helen smiled. 'I'll remember that, Constable.'

'Just doing my duty, Nurse.' He grinned. 'I'll be going then. Goodbye.'

'Goodbye, and thank you for coming along when you did.'

He rode away, and Helen got back into her car and drove on to town. She had a lot on her mind as she went to see Martin, and some of the problems concerned what she could tell him about it. She felt that the subject of Russell Thorpe had to be broached, although she felt chary of raising issues that might lead to a lot of needless worry on Martin's part. By the time she reached Doctor Arden's large house she had decided to say nothing at all.

Martin was in the driveway, watching a mechanic at work on his car, and he grinned when he saw Helen, coming towards her as she alighted.

'Sorry about this,' he said. 'Just one of those things. Good job it didn't happen while I was driving at speed. But it'll be fixed shortly.'

'So long as your life and limb were not in danger,' Helen said.

'It could happen to anyone,' he retorted. 'How are you?'

'Fine.' She thought of Russell Thorpe and then tried to bolt him out of her wondering mind. But she was still plagued by the problem of if she ought to tell him anything about the situation, and how much. She suddenly realized that he was staring at her, and when she tried to compose herself he nodded slowly.

'You've got something on your mind, my girl. Better get it off as soon as you can. Is anything wrong?'

'Nothing serious!' she smiled.

'That's why you're looking so seriously

worried! Credit me with a little commonsense, Helen. What's the trouble?'

'All right, I'll tell you. But not standing out here. Come and sit in my car while you're waiting for yours to be fixed.'

He nodded and went to the car, opening her door and settling her inside before going around to the other seat. He looked at her, nodding slowly, and Helen felt her throat constrict. The words wouldn't come.

'I'm listening,' he retorted. 'I thought it wasn't serious?'

'It's about Russell Thorpe!' Helen found it getting easier as she spoke the name.

'I thought it might be,' he replied, surprising her.

'Why?' She stared at him with a frown deepening on her forehead.

'I've been going around the villages as well. It's surprising how patients talk to their doctors or nurses. Treat them as confidants. I even heard about Thorpe kissing you in the fields on that Sunday evening you went out to his place for tea.' He smiled at her changing expression. 'That shook you, didn't it?'

'It certainly did. I was about to tell you the whole story, but it seems that someone had stolen my thunder. So you know! But who told you about it? Was it Russell himself?'

'No! Someone out doing a spot of shooting saw you together. I told you it's easy to gain a reputation around here.'

'Is that why you were so careful about kissing me on the side of the road?'

'That's right.' He smiled. 'But don't look so worried, Helen. It isn't the end of the road. I could tell by the way you've been trying to brush him off ever since that you have no feelings for him.'

'I want to tell you what happened. There's more to it than a few innocent kisses, Martin. It wasn't a case of being alone with a handsome man. I was practically hypnotized.'

'What?' He frowned. 'Go on. This is getting interesting.'

Helen began to explain, and went back to the first time she had met

Russell Thorpe. The words seemed to come easier after she had begun, and she stressed the strange power that Russell seemed to command. She finished by explaining what had happened on her way to town, and of the policeman's warning, and Martin's face was grim when she lapsed into silence.

'So that's the way of it. Thorpe wants a good talking to, and I've got a good mind to call on him the next time I'm passing.'

'Please don't, Martin,' she begged earnestly. 'The constable will be keeping an eye on things. Leave it like that. Now you know all about it there's no way he can make trouble between us.'

'I'll stay away from him,' Martin promised, 'but if he ever stops me to try his tricks then he'll get more than he bargains for.'

'I'm sorry about all of this, Martin.' Helen was serious as she faced him, and he smiled warmly and reached out to take hold of her hand.

'I don't see where you're to blame for anything, Helen,' he comforted. 'From what you tell me you're lucky it hasn't gone any further. But the next time you see him you'd better tell him exactly where he stands.'

'I've done that twice today already,' Helen said.

'Then tell him that if he doesn't stop pestering you he'll have me to contend with.' Martin spoke firmly, and Helen could see that he meant it. She smiled thinly.

'I can see that you would stand up for me,' she said. 'But there could be a lot arising from this. It would be better to let the policeman handle it.'

'I shall be thinking of you when you have to turn out in the small hours,' he went on. 'Your job is difficult enough without the extra worry of Thorpe in the back of your mind. If I see the constable about during my travels I'll have a word with him.'

'There's not much else he can do,' Helen pointed out. 'I am to ring him if I have to go out on a case during the night. He seems to have Russell

Thorpe's measure, if nothing else.'

'There must be something wrong with Thorpe,' Martin mused half to himself. 'I had a strange feeling or two myself when I went into the farmhouse to attend Mrs Farrell. I wonder if it would help to have a talk with her?'

'I doubt it. When I was there this afternoon she kept trying to talk me into giving Russell a chance. I think he completely dominates her.'

'I expect he does, from what you tell me of his hypnotic powers. Don't ever go there to the farm alone again, Helen. Promise me that. Even if it's in the middle of the night. Call me first and I'll meet you, or go in your place. Will you promise me that?'

'Gladly!' She nodded. 'Don't worry yourself about that, Martin. That place gives me the creeps.'

'That's settled then. Now let's forget about the whole thing and concern ourselves with a ruined evening.'

'But it isn't ruined,' she reproved. 'We're together, aren't we?'

'And that's the main thing.' He nodded, smiling at her. 'You always say the right thing, Helen.'

'All part of the service,' she retorted with a smile.

'Shall we go for a drive in your car? Mine will be all right where it is. I'm not doing anything to help by staying here, and we don't want to waste such a beautiful evening, Helen.'

'Hold tight then. I'll drive you for a change,' she replied.

Once again her worries over Russell Thorpe faded into nothing as she enjoyed Martin's company and sat in the car talking for what seemed hours, and as darkness returned Helen drove them back to town. When they arrived back at the spot from which they had departed Helen sighed deeply.

'Now I've got to go home,' she said.

'Are you worried about it?' He took her hands and held them tightly. 'My car is fixed now, I expect. 'I'll drive with you.'

'No, Martin, don't pander to my weakness. If I get called out at night I can't ring for you to accompany me. I don't think there will be any trouble.'

'I shan't be able to rest easy unless I know you are safely at home,' he retored. 'Just wait a moment and I'll get into my car. I'll lead the way, shall I?'

'All right, if it will make you feel any better,' she replied

He kissed her lightly on the mouth and got out of the car. Helen watched his tall figure as he walked into the driveway. She smiled gently to herself. She loved him! It was a satisfying emotion, and she knew it would grow still more deeply as time went by. But a frown creased her forehead as she thought of Russell Thorpe. She had a presentiment about him. He was going to try and cause trouble.

When Martin drove out on to the road and began to go through the little town Helen followed him at a distance. As she watched his car her thoughts turned over everything connected with Russell. She had told Martin everything, and he seemed to understand how it had happened, so there was no way in that direction where Russell could make trouble.

They approached the villages, and Helen kept glancing at the side roads, expecting to see Russell's car parked in wait, but she saw nothing suspicious, and realized that her nerves were giving her some trouble. When they arrived at the bungalow they got out of their cars and moved together, but Martin refused an offer to go in.

'Your mother is probably in bed already,' he said quietly. 'It is getting late, Helen. Put your car away and then go in. I'll see you sometime tomorrow.'

She tilted her face for a kiss, and he hugged her closely. She felt comforted by his presence, but could not help glancing around a little fearfully as she put the car into the garage. Martin walked to the door with her, and they kissed again before he pushed her firmly but gently into the house.

'Goodnight,' she whispered.

'Goodnight, Helen,' he replied, and

then he was gone.

She stood in the doorway until his car had departed, and when the sound of it faded along the lane she drew a deep breath. There was a moon showing through the trees at the bottom of the garden, and its soft light formed deceptive shadows. Helen stared around slowly, unable to suppress a shiver, and her imagination showed her a picture of Thorpe's Farm, lying silent and dark in the night. A breeze rustled through the trees, causing a sound that made her think of a dying person's last breath. Her nerves protested, and as she began to close the door her eyes caught sight of a furtive movement in the shadows by the gate. She froze, staring intently in that direction, and again she fancied that something moved down there. Suddenly she could imagine hostile eyes peering at her, and her nerves seemed to stretch and protest. She hurriedly stepped back into the house and closed the door, thrusting home the bolt and securing the lock.

For a moment she stood facing the

door, trying to get a grip on herself. This would never do, she told herself firmly. If she received a call now she would have to go out there to answer it, and losing her nerve wouldn't help in any way. But she waited by the door, her ears strained for any furtive sound that would reveal the presence of some prowler. In her mind there was a picture of Russell Thorpe, and she imagined it was he out there. She shuddered and made an effort to control her nerves, but before she went to bed she checked the security of the bungalow, and then lay in bed for some time with strained ears, just listening for any suspicious sound. She eventually fell asleep in a tense condition, and dreamed of many confusing matters. Subconsciously she longed for the morning and familiar reality . . .

11

When she opened her eyes next morning Helen looked around quickly, as if expecting to find some sign of trouble, but the sunlight was streaming in through the window, and outside the birds were singing and all seemed right with the world. She got out of bed and crossed to the window, opening it fully and leaning out to stare around that part of the garden which she could see. Had there been anyone prowling around in the dark? She shook her head when she failed to spot tangible evidence. She would have to maintain a tight grip upon her nerves if she were to face the nights with peaceful mind. She dressed slowly, trying to ease her thoughts away from the subject of Russell Thorpe.

Mrs Barclay studied Helen's face critically when they met in the kitchen. 'Didn't you sleep well last night, dear?'

she demanded worriedly. 'You're not looking your usual cheery self.'

'I had a mixture of confused dreams,' Helen replied. 'I didn't actually awake, but I wasn't resting easily.'

'Too much excitement, I expect. I can already sense romance for you and Martin. You're getting along very well together, aren't you?'

'Very well,' Helen echoed, glancing at her watch. 'I'll have to get a move on, Mother. Time is slipping away.'

'Russell Thorpe telephoned for you last night, Helen.' Mrs Barclay turned to the electric stove, and missed Helen's change of expression. 'It was rather late. He said Mrs Farrell was restless, and he wondered if you would go there to give her a sleeping draught or something.' She half turned to glance at Helen while keeping one eye on the toast under the grill. 'I told him there was nothing you could do, that he would have to send for Mrs Farrell's doctor. I don't like the way he's beginning to centre upon you, Helen. If he ever talks to you again you'd better make it quite plain that you want nothing to do with him.'

'I'll do that, Mother.' Helen had to make an effort to sound natural. 'What time did he ring?'

'About half an hour before you came in. I heard your car going into the garage.'

'Did you tell him where I was?'

'I didn't know exactly, did I? No, I said you were out for the evening and I didn't know when you'd be back.'

'Well that's all right. It's a fact that he does worry about Mrs Farrell.'

'That's something in his favour,' Mrs Barclay said firmly.

Helen half expected to get a call from Russell before leaving on her round, but nothing happened, and she went out to the car with a feeling of relief swelling inside her. The morning passed slowly, or seemed to, because her mind was dwelling upon the recent incidents. The fears of the night had receded, but she felt them vaguely in the back of her mind, like gathering storm clouds that would not disperse. By lunch, however, she was feeling almost normal, and when she went home she was humming to herself.

Mrs Barclay had lunch ready, and as soon as Helen sat down her mother began to give her some news.

'There was some trouble in the village this morning, Helen.'

'Really! What happened?'

'Russell Thorpe assaulted Mr Dagleish.'

'Assaulted!' Helen stopped eating and looked at her mother. 'Dagleish,' she commented. 'I seem to know that name.'

'She's the woman who is helping out at Thorpe's Farm while Mrs Farrell is laid up.'

'Oh yes! I'm with you. But what happened?' Helen's full attention was upon her mother now.

'It seems that Mrs Dagleish stole something from the house yesterday while she was working there, and Russell Thorpe missed it this morning. Instead of calling the police he went to

Mrs Dagleish's home and demanded the return of whatever it was. Mr Dagleish tried to throw Russell out of the house, and was struck down for his pains. The police were called, and Mr Dagleish has been taken to the hospital in Norwich.'

'Was it that serious?' Helen demanded. She felt a pang of fear as she watched her mother's intense face.

'It seems Russell lost complete control of himself,' Mrs Barclay went on. 'He left before the police arrived, and now they're looking for him.'

'What was stolen from the house? Money?'

'No. Mrs Dagleish denies touching anything, but it seems Russell accused her of taking a diary, or some papers from his study. She says she never went into the study. It seems a lot of fuss to make about nothing at all.'

Helen made no reply, and finished her meal, filled with a sense of anticipation that had her fingers trembling and her pulses racing. Was Russell displaying signs of a troubled mind? He must be under a strain of sorts, and that had shown in his actions the day before. He had accosted her in the evening after talking to her during the afternoon, and later he had rung the house for her. Then she thought of the shadow she had seen down by the gate after Martin had gone. She didn't like the way odd incidents were building up.

The telephone rang, startling her, and Mrs Barclay went in answer. She called out from the hall, and Helen went to take the call.

'It's Constable Godfrey,' Mrs Barclay whispered as she handed over the instrument.

'Hello,' Helen said clearly, although her throat was constricted. 'What's the trouble, Constable?'

'Can you come quickly, Nurse?' He sounded excited about something. 'We've got Russell Thorpe trapped in his house, but he won't come out, and he's got several guns. He wants to talk to you, and the Inspector thinks you ought to be here.'

'Good Lord!' Helen gulped in shock. 'Yes, I'll be along as soon as I can, Constable.'

'There'll be someone to meet you near the yard at Thorpe's Farm,' came the instructions. 'Please hurry.'

The line went dead, and Helen stood for a moment staring into space. She didn't stir until her mother questioned her. Then when she repeated what the constable had said her mind refused to accept any of it as fact.

'What on earth is happening, Helen? It sounds to me as if his mind has become unhinged. Are you going?'

'Of course.' Helen nodded, dragging herself from the inertia that gripped her. 'It's my duty to go in case anyone gets hurt. But will you put through a call to Martin and tell him about it?'

She was already moving to the door as she spoke, and her mother nodded. Helen went out and hurried to her car. She discovered that she was trembling violently, but it was all so incredible that she could hardly accept it. She drove along the lane, going much too fast, and had to caution herself firmly before her nerves gave her comfort. Her brain seemed frozen, and it was instinct alone that kept her driving the car properly.

When she reached the lane that led to Thorpe's Farm she saw a crowd of villagers there, being kept back by Constable Godfrey. She parked her car on the verge and got out, and the constable came towards her.

'The Inspector is up the lane by the farm gate,' he added. 'Go up, would you?'

Helen nodded, and started walking along the lane. She stared around as she went, telling herself that it had been about this time the day before when she had brought her mother here. What had happened to Russell in the meantime? She found that she was listening for the sound of shooting, but there were no disturbances. The birds were still singing and the sun shone brightly. It was a perfect late-Spring afternoon.

When she neared the farm gate she saw two police cars pulled into the side, and almost immediately a uniformed Inspector came out of cover and walked towards her. His face was grim, and Helen wondered what had been happening.

'Nurse Barclay?' he demanded as he reached her, and she nodded. 'Constable Godfrey has been filling me in with some of the details of your experiences with Thorpe. I've been in communication with him, and he's asked to be allowed to talk to you. I must warn you that he's armed, and seems to be mentally unbalanced at the moment. There's no telling what he'll do in a mood like that. From all accounts he's a strange man at the best of times.'

'Is Mrs Farrell still in there?' Helen demanded.

'Yes. She's the housekeeper, isn't she?'

'Yes. She's unable to walk.'

'Thorpe says she's all right, but he won't let anyone in to bring her out.'

'He thinks quite a lot of her,' Helen said. 'I don't think he would harm her.'

'Now how do you feel about talking to him?' The Inspector eyed her narrowly. 'Personally I don't know whether I ought to risk it or not. The sight of you may calm him, but on the other hand it might have the opposite effect. You have every right to refuse to place yourself in a position of danger, but I'd like to try something that might put a stop to all this before it goes any further. He hasn't used his gun yet, and until he does there's a chance that he may calm down and surrender without trouble.'

'What happened this morning to start all this?' Helen demanded.

'Thorpe accused his temporary housekeeper of stealing a diary, and assaulted the woman's husband when he went to get it back. Mrs Dagleish denies it, of course. Her husband has a fractured skull, so Thorpe hit him rather hard. We began to search for Thorpe and when Constable Godfrey came here to check Thorpe warned him off with a shotgun.'

'And he's asked to talk to me?' Helen demanded.

'That's right. I was summoned, and I've placed men around the farm with instructions to keep out of sight. I've called to Thorpe to put down his gun and come out to talk, but he refuses. Then he asked to see you.'

'I'll talk to him,' Helen said slowly. 'But how do I do it? Shall I walk out there in the open and call to him?'

'Good Lord no! We can't afford to take any chances, Nurse.' The Inspector shook his head emphatically. 'If you'll come with me I'll show you a way of getting close to the house without being seen. You can call from there. I'll stay with you, but remain out of sight. What I want you to do is reason with him, try to find out why he's doing this, and persuade him to give himself up before any real harm is done here.'

'I'll have a try.' Helen was surprised

to find that she was now quite calm.

'Come this way then.' The Inspector moved towards a hedge, and as Helen followed him they both heard the sound of a car coming along the lane. Helen paused when she turned and recognized it as Martin's.

'It's Doctor Reade,' she said.

Martin parked the car and got out hurriedly. His face was grim as he came towards them. Helen was pleased to see him. His presence gave her added comfort.

'Helen, you're not going anywhere near Thorpe, are you?' There was deep concern in Martin's tones. He reached out and took hold of her arm.

'Don't worry, Doctor,' the Inspector said. 'I won't let anything happen to the nurse. She'll keep out of sight.'

'I'll come with you,' Martin decided. 'This man Thorpe must be seriously unbalanced, Inspector, and I must warn you that he will be thoroughly unreliable in anything he says or does. Don't take him at his word.'

'I won't be making any mistakes, Doctor,' the policeman replied grimly. 'Come along and we'll see what we can do. I've got half a dozen men around the place, and they have their instructions. Thorpe doesn't know they're here.'

'I'm worried about poor Mrs Farrell,' Helen said.

They went through a gap in the hedge and followed it around to the side of the house. There was a barn and other out-buildings here, and the Inspector took advantage of the cover to lead them very close to the house. They paused by a hedge, and stood in the shelter of a low wall.

'I spoke to him from here,' the Inspector said, straightening a little to peer over the wall. 'Keep your heads down at all costs. Don't show yourself, Doctor. Anything could trigger him into action. We don't want a tragic ending to this.'

Helen agreed with that, and Martin put a comforting arm around her as they crouched out of sight. Helen stared around in disbelief. All this was too much to accept. She thought of her patients and the unfinished round, and knew that Martin, too, would have people to see.

'Thorpe, this is Inspector Helding again. Are you there?'

Silence followed the echoes of the Inspector's voice. Helen found that she was holding her breath, and Martin's arm was tensed about her shoulder. They waited while the Inspector repeated his call, and a few moments later Russell replied, his voice hesitant and almost unrecognizable. 'I have Nurse Barclay here as you requested. Do you still want to talk to her?'

'Not now. 'I've been thinking it over. It wouldn't do any good. Get her out of here. Take all your men away or I'll start shooting. I want to kill myself, and I've got to work up to it. I don't want to watch out for you. Clear off and leave me alone.'

'Is Mrs Farrell all right?' The

Inspector motioned for Helen to stay down, and he spoke in an aside. 'He's got a gun in his hands. It's not pointing in this direction, but we can't take any chances.'

'Mrs Farrell is all right.'

The Inspector crouched behind cover and shook his head slowly. 'You heard all that, I suppose. Now he doesn't want to talk to you, Nurse. You'd better get out of here, Doctor. It's going to be a long and nasty business, I'm afraid.'

'Wait,' Helen said as Martin made as to lead her away. 'Let me talk to him. I'm sure he can be persuaded to come out.'

'No. You heard what he said to the Inspector.' Martin kept a firm grip on Helen's wrist, holding her down in cover. 'He's really upset about something. What happened to spark this off, Inspector? The constable down the lane told me a little of it, but it hardly seems important to turn Thorpe like this.'

'There was a diary,' the Inspector said. 'All I can surmize is that there's something very important and personal in the diary. Thorpe has taken this line of action because he believes the diary has been stolen from him and the contents are now known either to the thief or to the police.'

'So it's likely that he's committed a crime of some sort and fears the diary will be used as evidence against him.' Martin nodded. 'I expect that's what has happened. It would need something of that magnitude to start him off.'

'Let me talk to him,' Helen said. 'It can't do any harm, can it?'

'All right.' The Inspector nodded. 'We've got to do something. The longer he's left on his own to brood over the situation the worse he may get. But keep your head down, Nurse, and if you see him turning the gun towards you then get down out of sight as fast as you can.'

Helen nodded slowly. Her throat was dry and she could hear the thumping of her heart. She slowly stood erect and gazed towards the nearby house. The Inspector pointed out the upper window where Russell had been, and Helen thought she spotted a movement back in the room.

'Russell!' she called, and heard her voice echo slightly. 'I want to talk to you. Will you answer?'

There was a silence, and Helen thinned her lips as she kept her eyes upon the window. She could just see over the wall, and her hands were pressed against the hard brickwork. Suddenly she spotted a movement at the window, and began to make out the features of Russell as he came closer to the window.

'Russell,' she went on. 'Is there anything I can do to help you?'

'You'd better get out of here before anything happens,' he replied in a loud voice.

'I'm sure there's no need for all this,' Helen continued. 'How is Mrs Farrell? Why don't you let someone come in for her?'

'She's all right here. She's lived here most of her life. She doesn't want to come out.'

'But she'll be frightened if she knows the police are here. Why don't you come and talk to them? The Inspector is here with me. He's an understanding man. You can explain what happened this morning.'

'It's too late. My diary is missing. That Mrs Dagleish took it. She was always poking around the house when she thought I wasn't here. Mrs Farrell warned me what she was like. She took the diary, and I expect she's handed it over to the police by now. That's why they're here. They want to arrest me.'

'I can assure you that no one has seen your diary, and I doubt if Mrs Dagleish took it.' Helen hoped she sounded convincing. 'I don't know what happened this morning at Mrs Dagleish's, but I'm certain it doesn't warrant this drastic action on your part. If you come out now to talk reasonably I'm sure this matter won't go any further.'

'You're wasting your breath,' came the terse reply. 'Get away from there, Helen. I don't want to see you.'

She saw a slight movement at the window, and the next instant the long barrel of a shotgun appeared. The Inspector, who was watching closely, dragged her down quickly. Martin put an arm around her, and Helen closed her eyes as she waited for the sound of a shot. But there was no disturbance, and she prayed inwardly with relief.

'Well that's that,' Martin said firmly. 'It's obvious that he's not going to listen to reason. You've got a big problem on your hands, Inspector, and I'm afraid there's nothing we can do to help.'

'That's how it looks to me, I'm afraid,' the policeman replied. 'Thank you for trying to help, Nurse, but now I suggest you take Thorpe's advice and get out of here. It might be safer for you.'

There was a sound at their backs and they turned quickly. A uniformed policeman, carrying a shotgun, appeared through the hedge, and Helen saw with some surprise that he was holding a large diary.

'What's this, Henderson?' the Inspector demanded.

'An old lady took advantage of the fact that you're keeping Thorpe busy around this side of the house,' came the terse reply. 'She threw this out of a bedroom window, and said Thorpe has threatened to kill her if we go in after him. I glanced in the diary as I came here, sir, and there's reason enough why Thorpe is acting this way, fearing that this has fallen into our hands. There's an account in it of how he strangled a girl and buried her out there in the fields.'

Helen froze in horror at the words, and the Inspector snatched the diary and eagerly began to scan through it. The silence that closed in about them was tense, and dragged at Helen's nerves. She wanted to scream to relieve the pressure building up in her mind, but she clutched Martin's hand and hung on desperately.

'Uhuh!' The Inspector looked up with narrowed eyes. 'We did get a report of a missing girl last year. So this is what happened to her. Keep it quiet for the moment, Henderson. If Thorpe learns that we do have his precious diary then we'll never get him out.'

'I might suggest that if you can keep him talking on this side of the house some of us might be able to get up the drain pipe to the window where the old lady is. If we get inside with her we can protect her, and make a try for Thorpe from there. There's no-one else in the house but the two of them.'

'It's worth a try in view of the evidence.' The Inspector nodded slowly. 'But I doubt if I'll be able to hold his attention. You could try, Nurse. He might listen to you. How long do you think you'll need to get into the house, Henderson?'

'Anything up to half an hour,' came the swift reply.

'All right, off you go. But remember that he's a dangerous man with that secret on his mind. Use only necessary violence to subdue him. Sergeant

Ransome is there with you, isn't he?'

'Yes, sir, and he's eager to make the attempt to get at Thorpe.'

'Very well. Off you go. We'll do what we can here to keep Thorpe occupied. Start talking to him again, Nurse.'

Helen nodded, and the policeman departed back the way he had come. Martin kept very close to Helen as she raised herself again. She called to Russell Thorpe, and after some moments he replied. Then began an ordeal of nerves for her. She could see Thorpe quite clearly, and the gun he was holding, and while she tried to engage him in conversation she wondered what was happening on the other side of the house. While she talked she heard Martin and the Inspector conversing about the situation. But she kept her attention upon the upper window and the shadowy figure that stood at it.

But after several minutes Thorpe began to lose interest, as if suspecting Helen's intention. Again he told her to get away, and then went from the window. Helen quickly informed the Inspector of the fact.

There followed a timeless period of waiting and wondering. The fear of bloodshed was very real. They listened intently, and when an outcry broke out in the house Helen turned away and cowered into Martin's arms. Not so the Inspector. He leaped over the wall and ran towards the house, calling for the rest of his men to follow him. When Helen raised her head to peer over the wall she saw that a downstairs window had been forced and a policeman was in the act of entering the house. But within a few moments a man's head appeared at the window where Russell Thorpe had been, and he signalled that Thorpe had been overpowered.

'We'd better go in and see if our services are required,' Martin said gently. 'You did very well, Helen. Come along. Mrs Farrell is in there, remember.'

They walked along the wall until they came to an open gate, and they entered the gardens of the house and walked to the now gaping front doorway. As they reached it two policemen appeared holding Russell Thorpe by the arms. He was ashen-faced and wild-looking, and Helen felt her heart turn over at the sight of him. But he made no comment, did not seem to recognize her as he was taken to a police car, and the next moment he was driven fast away.

Inside the house a policeman was carrying Mrs Farrell down the stairs, and the old lady was crying. She was placed upon a sofa in the big living room, and the Inspector waited to question her. Martin had come prepared with some drugs in his pocket, and he gave Mrs Farrell something for shock. Helen went to make some tea in the big kitchen. By the time she went back with the tea order had been restored. Mrs Farrell was making a statement to the Inspector, and Helen caught the tail end of it. She handed the old housekeeper a cup of tea.

'I did it for you, Helen,' Mrs Farrell

said slowly. 'I knew what happened to that other girl, who drowned herself, and Russell began talking about you, just like the strange girl he brought home one night. He couldn't think of anything else. He went out last night with the intention of bringing you here. I didn't want that to happen. You've been good to me, and your mother has. So I got his diary last night when he was out. I was going to give it to Mrs Dagleish this morning and ask her to hand it to the police. I knew they'd come for Russell if they read it. But he missed it before Mrs Dagleish arrived this morning, and it was lucky for me he suspected her of taking it and not me!'

'So that's what happened,' the inspector said. 'Well don't worry about anything, Mrs Farrell. You did the right thing. I'll have my men carry out an investigation. In the meantime Russell Thorpe will be held in custody.' He turned to Helen and Martin. 'I want to thank the two of you for your co-operation. It will be noted in my report.'

'We'd better be on our way now,' Martin replied. Helen?'

'Yes!' Helen wanted to get away from the house, but already the atmosphere seemed to be changing. She took a deep breath as she and Martin departed, and outside the sun was still shining from a cloudless blue sky. Inside her breast she was feeling a strange relief, and for the very first time since meeting Russell Thorpe those dark, background clouds that had worried her were gone. Whether it was the relief at knowing the premonition was removed or the fact that Russell was gone for a very long time at the least, she did not know. But as she glanced at Martin the love for him which she felt suddenly seemed to double itself, as if the whole of her mind could now focus upon him. She threw herself into his arms, startling him, but not for long.

'This is the start of something great,' he commented softly. 'I have the feeling that now the road is clear for the both of us, Helen. I love you very much!' He smiled. 'For ever and ever!'

'For ever and ever,' she repeated, smiling gently. 'That will be quite long enough, Martin.'

He gave her a lift down the lane to her own car, and the crowd was beginning to disperse. It seemed to Helen that she was awakening from a bad dream, and some of-the horror yet remained in her mind. But one glance at Martin's gentle face comforted her. While he was there in her life she had nothing to fear. Fate would see to that . . .

Other titles in the
Linford Romance Library:

EMERGENCY NURSE

Phyllis Mallet

Nurse Marion Talbot and Doctor Alan Vincent work together in Casualty. Marion is drawn to him a little more every day — but wonders what she can do to attract his attention. Then they each reveal they will have a relative visiting soon: Marion her mother, and Alan his uncle; and so they hatch a plan to give them a good time, while deciding to meet up themselves. But when a nurse from the hospital is attacked, and the police become involved, things do not run as smoothly as they had anticipated . . .

LONG DISTANCE LOVE

AnneMarie Brear

Fleur Stanthorpe, an Australian, arrives in Whitby to live out a dream after surviving cancer: opening a bookshop café before returning home after the summer. Only, she hasn't counted on meeting gorgeous Irishman Patrick Donnelly. He is looking for a solid relationship for the first time since his divorce five years ago — but she is having her last fling at freedom before going back to family and responsibilities. What will happen when the summer draws to an end and it's time for Fleur to leave?